ROSWELL HIGH

THE SEEKER

by

MELINDA METZ

POCKET
BOOKS

An imprint of Simon & Schuster UK Ltd. A Viacom Company
Africa House, 64-78 Kingsway, London WC2B 6AH

Produced by 17th Street Productions, Inc.,
33 West 17th Street, New York, NY 10011

Copyright © 1998 by POCKET BOOKS A division of Simon & Schuster

A CIP catalogue record for this book is available from the British Library

ISBN 07434 08802

3   5   7   9   10   8   6   4   2

Printed by Omnia Books Limited, Glasgow
First published in USA in 1998 by Archway Paperbacks.

"Hmm . . . I could wear this with those thigh-high tights I never wear," Maria DeLuca said softly to herself. She held the short, lime green dress up in front of her.

But then, hadn't she stopped wearing them because *nobody* wore thigh-high tights anymore? She tried to remember if she'd seen anyone at school in them lately.

Maria shook her head and glanced at the clock. "I am *so* late," she muttered. She was supposed to meet her five best friends at Flying Pepperoni soon. At the rate she was going, she'd never be ready in time.

"Maybe I should wear something blue," she murmured. It would make her eyes look even bluer. But Alex Manes, her best boy buddy, had told her that guys were lying when they said they loved a girl's eyes. She snorted. Alex would probably tell her she should show up in a teddy and high heels.

Maybe that's what it *would* take to get Michael Guerin's attention. Because admit it, she thought. That's why you've been staring at yourself in the mirror all morning. You're trying to figure out what will make Michael *notice*.

Maria's cat, Sassafras, nudged open the bedroom door

and leaped onto her bed. "Hey, Sass, you probably know exactly how I can make Michael realize I'm a g-i-r-l, right? Cats know everything—they just won't tell."

Maria picked up her gold chain—the one holding the ring she'd found at the mall last night—and looped it over her finger. She swung the ring back and forth in front of Sassafras's smushed-in Persian face. Sassafras pretended not to be interested for a minute. Then she shot out one paw. Maria caught a glimpse of something wet and red smeared across the pads.

"You're bleeding!" she cried. Sassafras must have been stalking through the rosebushes again, hunting birds. She was always getting herself scratched up that way.

Maria fastened the gold chain around her neck to get it out of the way. Then she snapped a leaf off the aloe vera plant she kept on her windowsill and squeezed the juice out of the leaf. She hurried over to the bed and gently picked up her cat's paw.

"This will make you heal faster," she told Sassafras.

The instant Maria's fingers made contact, it happened. The image of a robin flashed across her brain, making her want to chase it. The taste of milk flooded her mouth, delicious droplets running down her throat. She felt the sensation of warm sun on her back. And a hand scratching her under the chin.

Maria jumped back in surprise, releasing the cat's paw.

Sassafras leaped up onto the windowsill and sat there, tail twitching with annoyance.

Okay, that was totally weird, Maria thought. For a

second there I felt as if *I* was Sassafras. As if we had some kind of cat-to-human telepathy going.

Maria sat down shakily. The feeling she'd gotten when she touched Sassy—it was familiar. It felt like . . . like the connection she'd had with her friends. The connection the aliens—Max and Isabel Evans, and, of course, Michael—knew how to form. One night, right after she'd found out the truth about them, Max had brought Maria, Alex, and Liz Ortecho together with the three aliens. He wanted them all to trust one another, so he'd formed some kind of group connection.

It was as if the six of them linked minds. No, not minds. It wasn't that they knew each other's thoughts, exactly. It was that they knew each other's essences. We linked *spirits,* she realized.

And that's what had just happened between her and Sassafras. Which meant her cat's soul was made up of stuff like the taste of milk and the feel of sun on her back.

Maria smiled. Liz would laugh so hard if Maria tried to convince her that she had made a *connection* with Sassy. Her best friend would say it was just like the time Maria was *convinced* that she'd raised her IQ by taking ginkgo extract. Liz had finally done a chart for her, showing amount of ginkgo ingested versus Maria's test scores. The scores went up and down, while the ginkgo levels went up and up, proving that Maria had gotten a little carried away about the whole IQ thing.

It would be pretty cool if I really *could* connect with Sassafras, Maria thought. But the Liz Ortecho theory—that I have an extremely active imagination—is a lot more likely.

3

"Let's try this again, kitty cat." Maria headed toward Sassafras with the aloe vera leaf. "I just need to get a few drops on, and you'll be all set." She picked up Sassafras's paw and turned it gently.

Wait. Had she grabbed the wrong paw? There wasn't any blood on the pads of the paw she was holding. Maria looked at the other paw—no blood. She checked both paws again. No scrape or anything.

I know I saw blood on her, Maria thought. *That* definitely wasn't my imagination.

Maybe I healed her! The idea exploded in her brain like a skyrocket. That would be so totally and completely cool. Maria had been fascinated with healing practically her whole life. She knew her friends had trouble taking her aromatherapy and homemade vitamin capsules seriously, but Maria was absolutely convinced that her treatments worked.

One of the powers that Max, Michael, and Isabel had was the power to heal. She'd seen Max heal Liz when Liz got shot, and he had started by making a connection with her. So maybe Maria *had* made a connection with Sassy and then healed her.

Except, hello, you're not an alien, Maria scolded herself.

She needed to step back and think like Logical Liz for a minute. Okay, maybe Sassafras didn't have a scratch at all. Maybe she just had something red smeared on her paw, something that was now on Maria's bedspread or windowsill. There, that was a nice, logical thought.

Maria leaned over and braced her arms on her

dresser. "You have now reentered the reality zone," she told her reflection. At least she didn't look like an escapee from the loony bin. She looked perfectly normal.

Except . . . except there was something glowing through the thin material of her camisole. Right over her heart. Maria pulled the camisole down, fingers shaking.

It's the ring, she realized. She grabbed the chain and pulled the ring free. The stone set in the center was pulsing with purple and green light.

As she watched, the light faded. Maria sank down on the floor. She didn't think her legs would be able to carry her even one step. She held the ring up in front of her face and studied the stone. It looked sort of like an opal, with little shimmers of green and purple deep inside it.

Had she really seen it *glowing*? Or had that just been a trick of the light when she looked in the mirror? Or more of Maria's famous imagination?

But the glowing stone was the third weird thing in a row. First there had been the cat connection, then the disappearing blood. Even *my* imagination isn't that good, Maria thought.

Well, Liz would probably argue with that. She would be able to come up with a solid scientific explanation for everything that had happened.

Maybe getting all excited about seeing Michael gave me some kind of estrogen rush or something, Maria thought. I'll definitely have to ask Liz if rampaging hormones can cause hallucinations. Because that's all it was. A hallucination.

Right?

*　　　*　　　*

"So do you think Ray Iburg could be my dad or what?" Michael Guerin demanded. He swung himself into the passenger seat of Max Evans's Jeep.

Can you say pathetic? Michael asked himself. Don't bother saying hi. Or how's Isabel. Just start babbling about how you're so excited because last night you realized you might actually have a *daddy*.

At least Max wouldn't laugh at him. Max might *think* Michael was pathetic, but he wouldn't let it show. Actually, Max probably wouldn't even think it. Max was cool that way—one of the reasons the guy had been Michael's best friend practically forever.

That, and the alien thing. When you were one of only three aliens on earth—or at least when you *thought* you were one of only three aliens, like they had when they were kids—you pretty much had to be best friends with the other two. That would be Max and Max's sister, Isabel.

Max pulled off his sunglasses. His bright blue eyes gleamed with intensity. "I've been asking myself the same thing," he admitted. "I guess it's a normal thought—Ray *is* the first adult of our kind we've ever seen. Still, it's weird to think of anybody as my dad except, you know, my *dad*."

Michael hadn't even considered the possibility that Ray could be Max and Isabel's father. That would be so not fair. They already had two great adoptive parents.

Not like Michael. After he'd broken out of his incubation pod, a rancher had found him wandering in the desert and dumped him at the orphanage.

Michael had been doing his impersonation of a human pinball ever since, bouncing around from one foster home to the next.

Get over it! Michael ordered himself. You're becoming more pathetic by the second.

"You know, there are no laws against operating a moving vehicle while talking," he told Max.

"What? Oh." Max backed the Jeep out of the driveway of Michael's foster home du jour and headed toward the center of town. "We're both getting ahead of ourselves," he told Michael. "We don't even know if Ray is the same *species* as we are. All he said last night was that he's an alien, too. He could have come from a completely different galaxy or something."

Michael hadn't considered *that* possibility, either. He was really losing it. At least he hadn't bounded out to the car with seventeen Father's Day presents for Ray. He hadn't sunk to the complete depths of the Pathetic Ocean. Not yet, anyway.

"I guess you're right," he answered. "You know that blast-of-light thing Ray did to trap Valenti in the mall? I don't think we have the power to do anything like that. So maybe he is from *someplace* else."

Max—aka Mr. Responsibility—slowed down when the stoplight ahead of them turned yellow. Michael would have sped up.

"Or maybe we have powers that *we* don't even know about," Max commented. "Isabel said that . . . Nikolas could do a lot of stuff we can't."

Michael noticed Max's hesitation before he said Nikolas's name. He understood completely. Just

7

thinking of Nikolas started the acid churning in Michael's stomach.

"Maybe we *should* be hoping that Ray's a different kind of alien. Nikolas was from our home planet, and he almost got us all killed," Michael muttered. "We should never have let Isabel get near that guy. We knew she'd end up getting hurt."

"As if Isabel would listen to either of us," Max answered. He stopped at the stop sign on Smith Road for a full ten seconds—obviously having paid attention the day Mr. Brown covered the dangers of rolling stops in driver's ed—then continued down the empty street. "And anyway, we tried," he added.

"If Nikolas wasn't already dead, I'd want to kill him myself," Michael spat out, growing more furious with every word. "We warned him to stay away from Sheriff Valenti. We told him Valenti was dangerous."

"We didn't know Valenti would kill him," Max said in a low voice.

Michael didn't answer. No, they hadn't known the sheriff would go that far. It just proved how careful he, Max, and Isabel would have to be from now on.

"At least we got Izzy out of there without Valenti realizing the truth about *us*," Max said.

Michael was too angry to talk. He had known Nikolas was a stinking piece of scum. Isabel needed someone better, someone who could really love her the way she deserved. He should have done whatever it took to keep her away from Nikolas.

Max pulled up in front of the UFO museum. "Ray has an apartment on the top floor," he said.

"I can't believe you worked for the guy at the museum and didn't know the truth about him," Michael said as they circled around back. The first time he'd met Ray was last night, and that was only for a few minutes. He wondered if he would feel *something* from Ray today. Some connection.

Because he could really be my dad. The thought speared through Michael's brain before he could stop it.

When they got out of the Jeep, he dropped back a step so he was out of Max's sight, then wiped his hands on the legs of his jeans. He wished there was something he could do about the clammy patches spreading down his back and under his arms.

"Hey, it's not like alien auras look different or anything," Max answered as he led the way up the stairs to Ray's door. "How was I supposed to know?"

Max rang the doorbell and Ray opened the door a second later. "Figured you'd be here early," he said. "Where's everyone else?"

"Isabel's still pretty shook up," Max said. "She didn't want to come."

Michael was glad Max was doing the talking. His throat had gone completely dry—unlike the rest of his body, which kept pumping out sweat like he was running a marathon.

Ray ushered them into his living room. It was filled with beanbag chairs. And nothing else.

"What about the other three who were at the mall?" Ray asked.

Michael shot a quick glance at him. Max was right about Ray's aura. It didn't give any clue that Ray was *different.* It was shining white, with whorls of peaceful green and blue—the aura of a laid-back guy with nothing to hide.

"Uh, I didn't know if it was okay to bring them," Max said. "You know they're humans, right?"

Michael wanted to hear Ray's answer to this question. Would Ray think of humans the way Nikolas had? Nikolas had hated humans. That was one big sign there had been something wrong with him. He'd treated Liz, Maria, and Alex as if they were insects.

Ray laughed, and a few more green spots appeared in his aura. "I find humans quite enjoyable."

"So, who are you?" Michael demanded. His voice came out sounding hoarse and ragged. "Where did you come from?"

He hadn't been planning to ask that. He hadn't been planning to ask anything—not yet. At least I didn't use the *dad* word, Michael thought.

Ray pointed to his T-shirt. It said, I Survived the Roswell Incident.

"Wait. Are you . . . you were on the UFO that crashed back in the forties?" Max stammered. "We always thought . . . we thought our incubation pods came from that ship."

"They did. Anyone want a soda?" Ray asked. "I have some in the kitchen."

Michael felt like his head was spinning. Ray was on the ship with their incubation pods. So that meant he had to be from their planet. And it also meant that the odds that he was Michael's father had gotten much, much better.

Ray started toward the kitchen. Michael stepped in front of him, blocking him. "Wait. Back up," Michael demanded. "You knew about the incubation pods? So why didn't you come looking for us? Why weren't you there when we broke free?"

"Michael, ease off," Max murmured. "Ray's the guy who saved our butts last night."

"Don't tell me to ease off," Michael snapped. "This guy let us spend *years* not knowing who we are or where we come from or why we have the power we have. We had to stumble around, piecing it all together bit by bit. He didn't even bother to find out if we were alive or dead."

"I didn't have to come *looking* for you because I knew where you were," Ray explained. "I knew because *I* put you there. I put your pods in the cave. And then I left you alone. I thought it was your best chance for survival. I couldn't be sure that the government didn't know or at least suspect the truth about me, so it was safest for you to have no connection to me at all."

Michael felt his shoulders relax a little. "So are you . . ." He cleared his throat. "Are any of us related to you, or . . . ? I mean, are you our father or something?"

Michael held his breath as he studied Ray's face. Ray shook his head.

The air whooshed out of Michael's lungs. He felt like a deflated balloon. Too bad, he told himself. No daddy for little Mikey today. It's not like he really cared. Not much.

"The four of you—you two, Isabel, and the boy Sheriff Valenti killed last night—," Ray began.

"Nikolas," Max said.

"You were the children of some of the members of my team. We were scientists assigned to study earth to determine if it would be suitable for colonization," Ray continued. "If it was, we were going to form the first outpost here. But we quickly discovered that humans weren't psychologically ready to share their planet with an alien race."

"And our parents?" Max asked.

Now Michael was finally going to get the answer to the question, the question he'd been asking himself since he first understood what parents were.

"I'm the only survivor of the crash," Ray answered. "I'm sorry."

Michael felt tears sting his eyes. Oh, please. You've been assuming they were dead for years, he reminded himself. But when Ray showed up last night, Michael had started to hope again.

You're almost eighteen, he reminded himself. It's not like you're some little kid. It's not like you *need* parents. They'd probably just be a pain in the butt.

"So what happened that day?" Michael asked, struggling to keep his tone matter-of-fact. "What caused the crash?"

"Sit down, and I'll tell you," Ray answered.

Max and Michael lowered themselves into a couple of the beanbag chairs. Ray dropped down across from them, the greens and blues in his aura becoming mixed with gray. "We were going home," he told them. "The launch went smoothly. The team gathered at the observation window to take a last look at earth."

Michael noticed a patch of air in between him and Ray and Max begin to vibrate, shimmering the way it did coming off the pavement on really hot days. A blue-and-white basketball appeared in the patch of air, floating at eye level. The earth, Michael realized. How was Ray doing that?

"I thought we could use some visual aids," Ray said.

The earth shrank down to Ping-Pong ball size, and now Michael could see the observation deck and the team staring through the window at the planet. They fit the descriptions of the bodies witnesses had seen at the crash site—small, hairless torsos; long, thin arms; large heads with huge, almond-shaped black eyes.

Except none of the descriptions talked about their skin. How it was absolutely smooth, without even the tiniest wrinkle. And how it almost appeared metallic.

Michael felt his throat tighten as he studied the team members. They're all dead now, he thought. All except Ray. And they were so happy that day, so full of life.

Wait, where did that thought come from? Michael realized Ray wasn't just giving them pictures—he was giving them emotions, too. Michael could feel the pride the group of scientists felt in completing their job, their excitement about going home. And . . . and their pleasure that their children would be born there.

My mom and dad are in that group, he thought. Part of that excitement is coming from them. They really wanted me. He felt a hard, hot lump form in his throat. He swallowed, trying to get rid of it, but it remained lodged in place. They've been dead more than fifty years, he reminded himself.

"We didn't know that our prisoner had escaped," Ray continued. "Prisoner?" Max asked softly.

"His name was . . . well, it will be easier if I give him a human name. Let's call him Clyde—I never liked that name. Clyde was a stowaway when we left our planet," Ray explained. "He had stolen one of the Stones of Midnight—at least that's as close a translation as I can give you. The Stones are a source of tremendous power. Only the members of the consortium who govern our planet are allowed to use them. After Clyde stole the Stone, he managed to hide on board our ship. We discovered him on our way here and slapped him in a hibernation cylinder. We planned to leave him there until we could turn him over to the consortium."

"But when you were starting back, this Clyde guy escaped," Michael said. He didn't like the way this story was heading.

Ray didn't answer. Michael glanced at him and saw that his eyes were locked on the image of the team on the observation deck.

"I haven't looked at this one in a long time," he said. Michael had to strain to hear him. It was as if Ray was talking to himself. "I miss my friends," he added slowly.

He's all alone here, Michael thought. I have Max and Isabel and Maria, Alex, and Liz. But he's all alone.

Ray gave himself a little shake. "Yes," he told Michael. "Clyde escaped. I don't know how he did it, but he broke free from the hibernation cylinder, found the Stone, and came looking for us."

Michael leaned forward and watched as Clyde appeared on the observation deck. He looked just like the others, except he held a small stone that pulsed with a green-purple radiance. Two of the team members rushed toward him, but the stone shot out spears of sizzling light that knocked them to the ground.

"Dead?" Max asked. Michael already knew the answer. The grief and fury pouring into him from Ray's holographic image told him everything.

"Dead," Ray said. "He killed the rest of the team the same way. I don't know how I survived. Maybe he tried to kill too many of us at the same time. Even the Stones don't have unlimited power."

The image floating in the air changed to a single figure lying on the floor of the ship. Michael knew it was Ray. And he knew in that moment Ray had been near death. His aura had a deep ring of black around it.

"Clyde turned the ship back to earth. I'm sure he thought it would be a good place to hide out," Ray continued his story. "But he wasn't experienced in flying the ship. And he crashed."

The holographic image wavered, then disappeared. Ray rubbed his face with his fingers. "When I came to, I knew I didn't have much time. I was sure the hu-

15

mans would have seen the ship hit the ground. I hid your incubation pods in the cave. By the time I went back for the last one, the humans were already there. They had the whole ship surrounded. I couldn't get back inside, and I didn't want to lead them to you."

"So what did you do?" Max asked.

"I snuck away as fast as I could in the opposite direction," Ray said. "You know the rest. I opened the UFO museum . . . and waited for you to find me. If *you* approached *me,* I didn't think it would attract any unwanted attention."

"But how did you know it was us?" Max asked. "I couldn't tell you were an alien, so how did you know *I* was?"

"Well, I knew when you would break out of your pods, more or less," Ray said. "So I knew how old you'd be as a human. And also, I read your mind a little when you were working at the museum."

"What?" Michael cried. "We can't read minds!"

"Be patient," Ray told him. "I can teach you."

"Can you also teach us how to do *whatever* it was you did to stop Valenti?" Max asked. "If you hadn't helped us last night, he would've found out the truth about us all."

"I can try," Ray said. "But you are the first of us to have grown up on earth. I don't know how that will have changed your powers."

"Is the sheriff going to remember anything that happened?" Max asked.

I should have asked that question, Michael

thought. Valenti definitely had seen Liz in the mall last night. He probably had seen me and Maria and Alex, too.

"He probably lost at least five minutes of memory," Ray said.

That was cutting it pretty close. But it was enough. Valenti wouldn't remember much of what happened after he shot Nikolas. He wouldn't remember chasing them out of the mall.

Ray yawned. "I'm going to kick you guys out now. It took a lot of power to hold Valenti like that—I'm still wiped out." He grinned at them. "I'm not as young as I used to be."

Max frowned. "How old are you, anyway? How long do we live?"

Ray shrugged. "Time isn't measured the same way on our planet as it is here. And since we're on earth, our bodies may have adapted to age at a normal earth rate."

Michael studied Ray's unlined face. The guy didn't look a day over forty, but he'd been living here for at least fifty years.

Ray stood up. Max, always polite, stood up, too.

"Wait a minute," Michael said. "I want to hear the rest of the story. What happened to Clyde?"

"Dead," Ray answered. "I saw his body on my way to release your pods. Please, guys, I really have to rest."

Michael squinted at Ray's aura. Maybe talking about the crash had been too painful for him. The blue-green color was now covered with a net of deep

17

purple, something Michael had seen on people who had suffered a death in the family.

"Thanks," Max said, pulling Michael to his feet. "Thanks for everything."

"Yeah. You saved our lives—twice," Michael added. He headed to the door.

"Happy to do it," Ray said. "Come back anytime you want."

Michael hesitated with his hand on the doorknob. He turned back to Ray, but he couldn't quite bring himself to make eye contact. "Do you know if I have any brothers or sisters . . . back home?" he whispered.

Ray shook his head. "Siblings are rare on our planet," he said gently. "Each set of parents is only allowed one birthing cycle. Sometimes two children will hatch out of the same pod—"

"Like Isabel and me," Max interrupted.

"Yep," Ray answered. "But it happens very seldomly."

"Just curious," Michael said. Brothers and sisters probably would have been a pain in the butt, too, he forced the thought. He walked out the door without another word. Max followed him down the stairs. They climbed into the Jeep and stared at each other for a moment.

"So now we're supposed to head to Flying Pepperoni for pizza, right?" Michael finally asked. Yeah, that's what you did when you got absolute proof you had no family anywhere in the entire universe—went out for pizza.

"Right. We have to give a full report to Liz, Maria,

and Alex," Max answered. He started the Jeep and pulled out of the UFO museum parking lot. "I told Liz I'd pick her up on the way."

"Isabel should be with us for this," Michael said. "She'll want to hear about the crash and our . . . our parents."

"Um, she's not in great shape," Max admitted. "When I left the house, she was sitting in the middle of her bed. Just sitting there with the lights off."

"She wasn't cleaning out her closet or reorganizing her sock drawer or anything?" Michael asked.

Max shook his head, his expression troubled.

Michael frowned. He'd known Isabel since she was a little girl, and he knew that when she was upset, she didn't mope around or listen to sad music or even slam doors. She did things like arranging all her sweaters by color from dark to light, then arranging them all again by the kind of yarn they were made of.

"She's messed up in a big way," Max said. "I hated Nikolas, but he *was* her boyfriend. It's got to be hard to deal with watching someone you care about get killed."

"Then she shouldn't be alone," Michael said. If Izzy was in trouble, she should be with *him*. He wasn't going to let her sit by herself in the dark.

"She refused to come out of her room," Max told him.

"Drop me off at your house," Michael replied. "Pick up Liz, then come back. I'll have Isabel ready to go."

"I want us to be just friends," Max whispered as he drove toward Liz's house. "I love you, but we have to be just friends."

No matter how long he practiced saying it, it would never feel right. He didn't want to be friends with Liz. He wanted so much more.

"Being near me puts you in danger," he said loudly. "Look what Valenti did to Nikolas. He could do the same thing to you."

Now *that* felt a little better. Max would do anything to keep Liz safe. Anything to avoid feeling what Isabel was feeling right now.

Max turned onto Liz's street. He hoped Michael would have better luck with his sister than he had. Isabel had barely even looked at him when he tried to talk to her this morning. But if anyone could get through to her, it was Michael. Even when they were little kids, Izzy and Michael had always understood each other. It used to make Max jealous sometimes, but right now he was glad his sister had someone to talk to.

He couldn't read minds the way Ray could, but he could always feel the emotions of Isabel and Michael. And at the moment Isabel's pain was crashing down on him in never-ending waves. Michael must have felt it, too.

Poor Isabel. He was only getting the "lite" version of what she was going through, and even that was enough to make him feel sick. If he were in Isabel's situation, if Sheriff Valenti had shot someone he loved . . . if he'd shot Liz . . .

Max couldn't complete the thought. You're going to make sure that never happens, Max told himself.

"We have to be just friends," he tried out the sentence again. He pulled the Jeep into Liz's driveway. She was out the door in an instant—she must have been watching for him. He stared at her, wishing he could stretch this moment out and make it last the rest of his life. That's about how long it would take for him to get tired of the way the sun made Liz's long dark hair shine. The way that dimple in her left cheek deepened when she smiled at him. The way her low-slung jeans showed off the deep curve of her waist. The way—

Liz climbed in the Jeep and the moment ended. "Are you going to tell me everything now, or do I have to wait?" she asked.

"It's a pretty intense story," Max said. "I'd rather only tell it once, okay?"

"Are you all right?" she asked. She rested her hand lightly on his arm, and Max's breath caught in his throat. He bet kissing any other girl in school would have less effect on his body than that one simple touch from Liz.

"Yeah," Max answered. He knew he had to say

something to her. But right now the only thing he could think of was her hand on his arm. Her soft skin touching his, sending waves of heat through his body. He had to get away from her hand. Then he would be able to function, able to do something other than imagine how it would feel to take her in his arms. . . .

He reached into the glove compartment and pulled out a pack of gum. He didn't want gum. He just wanted a way to move his arm out from under her hand without looking like that's what he was doing.

"Um, I wanted to talk to you about what happened last night," he said in a rush.

A deep flush crept up Liz's throat and spread to her cheeks. He knew exactly what she was thinking about—their cramped little hiding place under the counter at Victoria's Secret.

Liz had had to lie on top of Max, her body stretched out against his. He knew he shouldn't have touched her. He knew that was breaking the rule—the just-friends rule—but he hadn't been able to resist running his fingers over her face. Tracing her perfectly arched eyebrows, her sharp cheekbones, her soft lips.

When she had started touching him back, he'd had no choice but to wrap his hands in her thick silky hair and kiss her. A kiss that totally moved him. They had kissed before that night. Three kisses. Max remembered each of them, had gone over them again and again in his mind, trying to relive them. But this last kiss . . . it took them to a whole other level of kissing.

Max yanked his thoughts back to the present.

"I just wanted to say that . . ." Max hesitated. "I wanted to say that even with what happened, I still don't want to . . . I still think we should keep on as friends, as just friends. It's too dangerous for you otherwise. If you get close to me, Valenti gets close to you."

"Max—" Liz reached out for him again, her eyes concerned.

Max jerked away from her. "Last night Valenti *proved* how dangerous he is," he interrupted. "He shot Nikolas. Isabel said he didn't even ask any questions first. He just pulled out his gun and blew Nikolas away."

Max stole a glance at Liz. Her beautiful dark eyes shimmered in the sunlight. Shimmered with *tears,* Max realized.

He wanted to pull the car keys out of the ignition, hand them to her, and beg her to stab him through the heart a couple dozen times. That would be a lot less painful than having her look at him the way she was looking at him right now—like he had hurt her more than she'd realized she *could* be hurt.

"I didn't mean to confuse you or mess with you or anything," Max added quickly. "The situation just got out of control. I won't let it happen again, I promise."

"You promise," Liz repeated dully.

He waited, but she didn't say anything else.

I won't have to worry about keeping that promise, Max thought. After the way I just destroyed her, Liz will never *let* me touch her again.

*   *   *

"Did you just take a sip of my orange soda?" Alex exclaimed.

"Huh?" Maria glanced down at her hand and realized she was holding Alex's glass. "Oh. Sorry," she mumbled. She slid it across the table to him.

"No, go ahead and finish it," Alex said. "Flying Pepperoni has the best orange soda in town. I just didn't think a natural foods baby like you would appreciate the perfect blend of sugar, water, and artificial colors and flavors."

"I thought I was drinking my mint tea," Maria admitted. Her mind was a million miles away. Actually, that wasn't true. Her mind was right here in Roswell—over at Ray Iburg's. "Do you think there might be a whole *community* of aliens in Roswell?" she asked Alex.

"They do seem to be popping up all over the place lately," Alex answered.

Maria ran her finger around the rim of her cup, collecting all the drops of moisture. "Everything's going to change," she murmured.

Alex looked alarmed. "Why?"

"Well, if there's this whole group of aliens, Michael, Max, and Isabel are going to want to be a part of it," Maria said. "And we can't be a part of that."

"But . . . but Isabel needs us," Alex said urgently. "They won't just drop us the minute they find other aliens. They *won't*."

Maria shrugged. "Still, it won't be the same." She stared into her tea. What would she do without Max joking around with her, calling her pea pod? Or

Isabel's hilarious fashion critiques of everyone who walked by in the quad? Or Michael crawling through her window late at night just to hang out?

Yeah, that's what she would miss the most. But if Michael found out there was a whole assortment of alien girls available to him, it's not like he'd still be showing up at Maria's every couple of nights. She was your basic, ordinary human chick. How could she compete with girls who would have so much more in common with Michael, girls who would share his species memories of his home planet? Girls who were probably totally beautiful in some exotic, enticing, non-cute-girl-next-door kind of way.

"Why is everyone so late?" Alex complained.

"Ray must have had a lot to say," Maria answered.

"So what's your excuse?" Alex asked. "You were late, too."

Maria wondered if Alex was having the same kind of thoughts she was—except about Isabel, not Michael. That would explain why he was getting so annoyed.

"Alex, you have to be at least fifteen minutes late for it to count," Maria explained. "Plus I have a great excuse. My clock is doing something weird. When I was getting dressed, it skipped ahead, like, five minutes in one jump."

"There they are. Finally," Alex announced.

Maria glanced over her shoulder, her eyes going directly to Michael. His face wasn't giving any clues about how it had gone at Ray's. He'd shoved whatever emotions he was feeling way down.

Michael slid into the booth next to Maria. He pulled Isabel down next to him and looped his arm around her shoulders. Maria didn't know what she was supposed to think about that. He chose to sit next to *her*, which was good. But he had Isabel pulled up close against him, which was—

Get over yourself, Maria thought. Isabel just went through something world shattering. That's what you should be thinking about. Not whether Michael's sitting closer to you or her. Maria rummaged around in her purse and pulled out a vial of tangerine oil. She reached across Michael and held it out to Isabel. "I like to smell this when I'm . . . not feeling so great," she said. "I want you to try it, okay?"

Isabel didn't answer. Her blue eyes were focused on the sugar shaker in front of her. She's trying not to cry, Maria realized. She'd never thought of Isabel as a crying kind of girl. Isabel was so strong, the kind of person who didn't take anything from anyone. But it was like the steel inside her had turned into glass, glass so fragile, a puff of air could shatter it.

Maria pressed the tangerine oil into Isabel's hand and gently closed her fingers around it. "Take it home and try it later," she said. "If you like it, I'll get you some more."

"Thanks," Max said. Maria smiled at him, although she had to fight to keep the smile in place when she got a good look at his face. He looked . . . ravaged. That's the only word that seemed to fit. This isn't just about what happened last night, Maria realized. There's something new. Something horrible.

She glanced over at Liz. Liz sat with her arms wrapped around herself. It was like she was trying to take up as little space as possible. Or like she didn't want to have one inch of her body touching Max's.

What was going on? Had Max already told Liz whatever he found out from Ray this morning—was that why she looked like she was about to throw up?

"Somebody better start talking fast," Alex said.

Max pulled in a deep breath. "Do you want to do this or do you want me to?" he asked Michael.

"You're our fearless leader. You do it," Michael muttered.

Maria didn't like the sound of his voice. It was too flat, too dead sounding.

"Okay, so we went over to Ray's this morning," Max began.

"Did any of you start writing that history paper?" Alex interrupted. "Don't tell me yes, because I haven't even picked a topic."

What was he talking about? None of them were even *in* his history class. Maria opened her mouth to ask him if he'd lost his mind, but then she heard footsteps coming toward them, and she caught a whiff of cologne. She knew that smell. She didn't have to turn around to know that Sheriff Valenti was behind her.

What was he doing here? Did he know the truth about Michael and the others? Maria felt a shiver race across her shoulders. She hoped Valenti didn't notice. She didn't want to do anything that might make him suspicious.

"I'm already halfway done with my paper," she

27

told Alex. "You shouldn't be here right now if you haven't started. You should be at the library."

Valenti stepped up to the table. "I'm looking for Nikolas Branson," he announced. "His parents called me this morning and informed me that he never made it home last night."

Did he sound this calm when he talked to Nikolas's parents? Maria thought wildly. Did he just ask them all the usual questions and tell them he'd do everything he could—knowing the whole time that Nikolas was dead? Dead because of *him!*

"Nikolas didn't seem like the kind of guy who would be tucked in bed by midnight, you know what I mean?" Liz said, looking Valenti right in the eye. "He probably just partied a little too strenuously last night."

"Yeah, I bet he'll come rolling home sometime this afternoon," Alex agreed.

Valenti turned to Isabel. "Is that what you think?"

"Sounds like Nikolas to me," she said. Her voice gave the tiniest quiver when she said her boyfriend's name, but she answered without hesitation. She must have a little of her steel left after all, Maria decided.

"Is that all you can tell me? The two of you were together last night, weren't you?" Valenti asked. "My son, Kyle, said you and Nikolas were going out."

Thank you, Kyle, Maria thought. The little rat boy had to tell his father everything about everyone at school.

"We were together for a while, but we . . . we had a fight. I . . ." Isabel's breath began coming in ragged pants.

Maria shot Alex a panicked look. Isabel was going

to lose it, right in front of the sheriff! What should we do? she thought frantically.

Michael grabbed a napkin from the dispenser and shoved it at Isabel. "Thanks for getting her started again," he snapped.

"We've been trying to cheer her up," Maria jumped in. "Nikolas was a complete jerk to her last night."

Isabel buried her face in her hands. Michael pulled her against his chest and glared up at Valenti.

"Well, if you hear from him—any of you—I expect you to call me immediately," Valenti told them. He turned and strode away.

Silence stretched out at the table. Maria didn't even hear anyone breathing. She knew she wasn't.

"Okay, he's gone," Max finally announced. Maria let out her breath in a whoosh.

Isabel sprang to her feet. "Give me the keys, Max. I'm going home."

"Izzy, come on, stay with us," Max said.

"No! I can't stay here." Isabel's voice rose higher and higher. Maria noticed her getting some curious looks from the people in the next booth.

"One of us could go with you," Liz volunteered.

"Or we all could," Maria added.

"I need to be alone," she snapped. "All of you just stay away from me." Max pulled out his keys, and Isabel snatched them out of his hand.

Maria watched as Isabel half ran out of the place. Doesn't she know that now is when she needs us the most? Maria thought.

*   *   *

29

Isabel chipped a little more wild cherry nail polish off her big toe. She added the tiny red flakes to the pile on her bedspread. She should never have let Michael coax her into going to Flying Pepperoni. She needed to be here, in her bedroom, where she could work on her little nail polish mountains. As long as she kept chipping and piling, she could blank out and turn the inside of her head into a buzzing gray screen.

But when she stopped, the screen got clear and a little movie began to play. A movie of Sheriff Valenti shooting Nikolas. Over and over and over.

The movie theater in her head was ultra-high-tech. It even came with odorama. Every time she heard the shot, she smelled the gunpowder, the odor of a row of firecrackers set off all at once. The sharp scent of her nail polish wasn't nearly strong enough to block it out.

Nikolas had always said humans were like insects. He'd said if Valenti got too close, he'd just squash him. And Isabel had believed him. She'd started thinking she had no reason to be afraid of the sheriff. That she had wasted years being terrified of a man whose powers were no match for Nikolas's or even her own.

But Nikolas was the one who had gotten squashed last night. Leaving behind an ugly spot on the floor, like any good bug. And now Isabel remembered why Valenti had filled her nightmares since she was a little girl. She remembered that she would always be hunted and that she would never be truly safe.

Isabel chipped another piece of polish off her toe and carefully added it to her little mountain.

She glanced at the clock. Max wouldn't be back from Flying Pepperoni for at least an hour. But as soon as he got home she knew her brother would be wanting to talk, wanting to tell her whatever they found out from Ray. As if she cared. As if she wanted to know anything more about her history, her stupid alien powers. If she were just a normal girl, none of this would have happened.

Isabel chipped the last speck of polish off her big toe. She carefully added the red flake to the very top of her mountain and studied her feet. Not one dot of color left. She grabbed her bottle of nail polish and started to paint them again. She worked fast, not worrying about being sloppy. She wanted to get her toes painted and dry so she could start chipping and piling again.

She heard footsteps coming up the stairs. Max must have followed her from Flying Pepperoni, worried about his baby sister. She wished he'd leave her alone. Him and Michael and everyone else.

A knock sounded on her bedroom door. "Go away, Max," Isabel said.

"It's not Max—it's Alex. Can I come in?"

Isabel sighed. She couldn't deal with Alex right now. If she stopped focusing on what she was doing, the movie in her head would start back up. She knew it. And she wouldn't be able to take it. She couldn't watch Nikolas die again.

"Your mom gave me some ginger ale and saltines

to give to you," Alex called through the door. "She said your stomach was upset."

She really did *not* want to talk to him. Maybe if she didn't say anything, Alex would go away. She finished painting her last toe. She grabbed a magazine and fanned her feet. She wanted the polish chippable—now. Then she could get the movie to stop.

"It's too late to pretend you aren't in there," Alex announced. "You already said something."

"Did someone invite you over here?" Isabel snapped.

Alex was probably getting sad little puppy eyes on the other side of the door. But too bad. She *hadn't* invited him.

"Nope. I know I'm always welcome," Alex answered.

Isabel tested the polish on her toes. Still too wet to chip. "What? What do you want? Do you want me to tell you that you were right about Nikolas?" she demanded. "Okay, you were right. He was dangerous. He almost got us all killed. You know everything. Okay? So go."

She heard the doorknob turn, heard Alex mutter a curse when he discovered it was locked. "That's what you think?" he exploded. "You think I came over to get my jollies off making you tell me I was right all along?"

Good, Isabel thought. Get mad and get out. She waved her hands over her toenails. Almost done. Almost.

Alex sighed. "Why is it always so hard with you?" he

mumbled. "Let me spell it out. I came because I wanted to see if you're okay. You went through something pretty traumatic. I thought you could use a friend."

Oh, great. Now he was going to be nice to her. She couldn't take it. She and Alex . . . they had something sort of nice starting up before . . . before Nikolas came to town. But Nikolas had totally blinded her to everyone else.

Isabel's eyes filled with tears. How was she going to survive without him? She didn't have one thing to remember him by. Not one picture. Not anything. She wished she could have that ring he always wore, the one with that strange stone. She could hold it in her hand and at least know that it was something Nikolas had touched. Something Nikolas had . . . had . . .

Isabel's throat began to burn. She felt a tear slide down her cheek. Nikolas . . . oh, God, Nikolas . . .

The smell of gunpowder flooded her nose. She scraped at her toenails, trying to block out the image of Nikolas dying. But the polish wasn't dry enough to chip. It smeared across her fingers, wet and red.

Isabel choked back a sob. What was she going to do? She'd go crazy if she couldn't make the screen go blank.

"I'm not leaving," Alex said, his voice quiet. "Yell at me. Give me your ice princess thing. Whatever. I'm not leaving. If you don't want to talk, fine. I'll talk. I'll tell you about my champion Little League season, for starters. One of the best times ever. I can still smell the grass in the outfield. And taste that flat purple taffy from the snack shack . . ."

Alex kept talking. And his voice, his voice made the screen go blank.

Isabel stood up and crept over to the door. She sat down and leaned her cheek against the door. Listening to Alex describe every moment of the very first game of the season.

He was so normal. A nice, normal guy.

She wished she could be normal like him. A nice, normal girl who couldn't see auras or dream walk or heal. A girl who didn't ever wake up screaming from dreams of Sheriff Valenti with the eyes and teeth of a wolf, a wolf intent on hunting her down.

I can be normal. I'll be just like Alex. I'll never use my powers again, she decided. Never.

Michael glanced at his alarm clock. Ten-thirteen. He'd only been in bed for thirteen minutes. It felt like thirteen days. He wasn't tired. At all. He only needed two hours of sleep a night—one of the cool things about not being human—and he wouldn't even be needing those two until later.

But ten o'clock was his bedtime. His *bedtime*. He could not *believe* he had a bedtime. Mr. and Mrs. Pascal thought that structure was the key to making children feel happy and secure. Or some stupid psychobabble like that.

His new foster parents had rules for everything. They had given him a typewritten list with a dorky little drawing on the top—a raccoon that had one of those cartoon balloons coming out of its mouth. The raccoon was saying, "Rules for Pascals' Rascals."

The rules were in the form of a poem. "Please lower the toilet seat. Wash your hands before you eat." That kind of thing. Alex had practically wet his pants laughing when Michael showed it to him.

But there was nothing funny about the rules when you had to follow them. And Michael did. At least for a while. His social worker, Mr. Cuddihy, would have a hissy fit if he got a complaint call during Michael's first week at a new place. So that meant no sneaking out of the house for a few weeks.

Which meant no late night visit to the Evans house. Michael wanted to check up on Isabel. He felt like shaking her for wasting one tear on Nikolas. But he also felt like holding her tight and letting her cry as much as she wanted. He'd do whatever it took to get *his* Isabel back—smart-mouthed, sassy, stuck-up Izzy, not that pale sad-eyed girl who'd been sitting next to him at Flying Pepperoni.

Tomorrow, he promised himself. I'll get there first thing in the morning, score some breakfast, and see if Isabel needs me.

He rolled over onto his side. The covers were tucked in too tight. He felt like a mummy. He gave them a yank, but it didn't help. The kid in the next bed—Dylan—gave a high, whistling, wheezing snore. Michael pulled his pillow over his head.

Down the hall he heard the baby begin to cry. A moment later he heard Mrs. Pascal's bunny slippers flapping down the hall.

I would kill, Michael thought, or at least maim, to get out of this house. I could just crawl out the window and go. I don't need to go to Isabel's. I could go somewhere else. I could go . . . to Maria's!

Yeah, that was perfect. Right now he just wanted to kick back—and Maria's girlie-girl room was the place to do it. He liked the way she had clothes and nail polish and all her little vials of perfume oils scattered everywhere. He even liked the weird way her room smelled—like roses and cough drops.

Even when Maria wasn't home, he liked to hang there. But it was better when she was there. Maria could always make him laugh. A lot of times she wasn't even trying to be funny, like when she was getting all earnest about her aromatherapy.

Mrs. Pascal started to sing to the baby. It cried louder. Michael didn't blame it. Mrs. Pascal's voice . . . well, she better keep her day job, that's all he had to say.

Michael stifled a groan. I can't take it, he thought. I'm not going to live until morning.

"Sleep, don't peep, don't creep, don't beep, don't seep," Mrs. Pascal crooned.

Seep?

"Just dream, dream, dream, dream, dream, dream, dream."

Dream walking, Michael thought suddenly. That's what he should be doing. Just because he couldn't fall asleep himself didn't mean he couldn't go into someone else's dreams.

Michael closed his eyes and took a few deep breaths. Mrs. Pascal's singing grew fainter, and so did Dylan's snoring. He took one more breath, and the dream orbs became visible. The glistening, soap-bubble-iridescent orbs swirled around him. Each gave off one pure note of music. Big improvement.

Michael didn't dream walk nearly as much as Isabel did. But he'd still spent enough nights channel surfing through the dream orbs to know which orbs belonged to which people at school.

Doug Highsinger's orb spun past. Doug was usually having some kind of sex dream. But watching a football star get off wasn't Michael's idea of fun. Pass.

Arlene Bluth's orb whacked him on the back of the head. He definitely didn't want to go exploring in her dreams. She only dreamed about school. Right now she was probably having a nightmare about taking a test with a number *three* pencil. Pass.

Tim Watanabe's orb was a pass, too. Big pass. For some reason Tim Watanabe kept dreaming about a big clown with a green tongue named Bobo. It was none of Michael's business, but he didn't think a little therapy would hurt that boy.

Michael caught the sound of a high, sweet note of music. Maria's orb. He grinned. He couldn't go hang out in Maria's room. But he could visit one of her dreams.

Except it was kind of weird going into a friend's dream, like barging in on them in the bathroom or something. Sure, he'd gone into Maria's dreams a few times. But that was before he really knew her. It felt different now.

I'll just tell her I'm there, he decided. Then it won't be like I'm spying on her.

He began to whistle, drawing her dream orb to him. It whirled into his hands, soft and cool under his fingers. Michael drew his hands apart, and Maria's dream orb expanded. When it was big enough, he stepped inside.

Maria lay in a field of wildflowers. Doing some major making out with a dark-haired guy.

Whoa. *Not* what he expected. Michael backed out of her dream—fast. He'd thought Maria would be dreaming she was a bird or a mermaid or something. Those were the kinds of dreams he remembered her having.

Those were the kinds of dreams she *should* be having. Maria dreaming about boarding the love train with some guy—that just didn't feel right. And who was that guy, anyway? Michael had only gotten a glimpse of him, but he didn't look familiar. Was he someone from school? Did Maria have some kind of major crush going?

Michael sat up in bed, chewing on his lip. Maybe he should check it out. Maria had no concept of what guys were really like. She didn't know that they— some of them, anyway—lived to scam girls like her. Sweet girls. Innocent girls. Yeah, he should make sure Maria wasn't getting all gooey over some total jerk-off.

Michael closed his eyes and called Maria's dream orb back over to him. He coaxed it into expanding, then stepped inside. Maria and the guy were still going at it. He couldn't quite see the guy's face, though. Maybe that's because half of it was down Maria's throat.

Michael did not like this. At all. He moved closer, circling around Maria and the sex fiend. They didn't notice. They wouldn't notice a nuclear explosion right now.

No guy should be doing *that* with Maria. Maria was the girl Michael watched stupid horror movies

39

with. Maria was the girl who insisted on teaching him how to bake a cake. Maria was the girl who made him wear an *apron*. Maria was his buddy. She should not be kissing some guy. It was just wrong. So wrong.

It's a dream, he reminded himself. Dreams are weird. Dreams aren't always about what you wanted. Maria probably has no interest in that guy or any guy.

It's not like Arlene Bluth *wanted* to take tests with the wrong pencil. It's not like Tim Watanabe wanted to live in a doghouse with Bobo the green-tongued clown. It's not like Doug Highsinger wanted to bed half the girls at—

Bad example.

"Do you think guys have some kind of on-off switch in the back of their heads?" Liz asked. "I mean, I've never seen it in any diagram in a bio textbook, but I'm really thinking it has to exist."

Liz tried to keep her tone light. Maria was her best friend, but that didn't mean she wanted to listen to Liz cry over Max every moment of every day.

Maria didn't answer. She sat on the low wooden bench in front of her locker, holding one of her sneakers. She kept staring at it as if she'd forgotten what it was.

Liz took the sneaker out of Maria's hand and stuck it in her locker. "We take the gym clothes off, then we put the street clothes on, then we leave school and go home," Liz said in her best kindergarten teacher voice. "At the speed you're moving, we might as well spend the night in here. Everyone else is already gone."

"Sorry," Maria mumbled. "I was spacing. What did you ask me?"

That was so unlike Maria. Maybe some people spaced out once in a while when their friends were talking to them. Even their best friends. But not Maria. She had the gift of listening with almost maniacal attention.

"I wanted to know if you think guys have a hidden on-off switch," Liz answered. "Something that makes them kiss, totally, completely kiss you one day and then treat you like the girl who works behind the counter at some convenience store the next day. Some girl they say hi to when they buy pork rinds. Some girl whose name they don't even really know. Some girl who looks sort of familiar. Some girl—"

"Stop," Maria begged. "I not only get the picture, I get the whole photo album. You. Max. He loves you. He loves you not. Do you want to hear my theory?"

"Please." Liz grabbed her brush from the top shelf of her locker. She whipped it through her long dark hair.

She hoped Maria could help her figure this out. She couldn't stop thinking of that kiss. That incredible kiss. Every time her mind touched on it . . . whoa. It was like her stomach dropped down to her toes and bounced back up again. A scientific impossibility, yes. But that's how it felt.

"I just don't understand how Max could kiss me like that and then shove me away," she muttered. "Unless . . . unless maybe he doesn't feel the same things I do. But I mean, he was *trembling* when I touched him."

41

"Hello? I'm giving my theory," Maria reminded her.

"Sorry." Liz took a deep breath. "Shoot."

"Okay. First, I think Max is totally and completely in love with you," Maria said.

"But then why—," Liz began to protest.

"Wait, I'm not done." Maria pulled off her other sneaker and tossed it in her locker. "Second, Max thinks the closer you get to him, the more danger you're in. So he pushes you away and treats you like you're the girl who sells him pork rinds to keep you safe. It's actually sort of sweet."

"But I don't care about being safe." Liz brushed her hair so hard, it crackled. "All I care—"

"I'm still not done," Maria interrupted. She pulled off her gym shorts and pulled on a long saffron yellow skirt. "Third, the kiss. The important thing about the kiss is when and where it happened. Sheriff Valenti was this close to finding you. You were in a we-could-die-any-second kind of mode. And when you think you're going to die, you do things you wouldn't usually do."

Liz threw her brush back in her locker and slammed the door.

"So all I have to do to make Max kiss me again is to almost get myself killed."

Maria pulled off her T-shirt. "Yeah. So next time try and almost get killed somewhere where there's candlelight, maybe some music. Somewhere romantic."

Liz tried to smile. But if Maria's theory was correct, and it made total sense to Liz, then Max's on-off switch was pretty much locked in the off position.

Maria reached for her camisole. Liz caught sight of a ring on a chain around her neck. "Nice," Liz said, reaching for it. "What kind of stone is that?" The color shifted from purple to green and back with each movement Maria made.

"I'm not sure exactly," Maria answered. "I've never seen one like it." She pulled on her shirt, slid her feet into her sandals, and grabbed her purse. "Let's get out of here." She led the way out of the locker room.

"So do you think I should send Valenti an anonymous note?" Liz joked. "Tell him he can find Max at one of those dark tables at the Rings of Saturn restaurant, where I'll just happen to be, too, doing the just-friends thing?"

"That's one possibility," Maria answered as they crossed the polished wood floor of the gym. "Or, and I know you're not going to like this . . ."

There were times when Liz knew exactly what Maria was going to say before she said it. This was one of them. "You think I should go out with other guys," Liz said before Maria could. The words hurt coming out of her mouth.

"Got it in one," Maria answered. "There's more to life than getting straight A's and raking in the tips at your dad's restaurant. You should have some fun."

"Like you're out with a different guy every night of the week," Liz teased. Maria wasn't exactly a party girl lately, either. And Liz thought she knew why. Liz had known Maria since the second grade. She'd seen her go through some major crushes. But she'd never seen her look at a guy the way she looked at Michael.

And Maria hadn't said a word about him to Liz. That meant she felt something big. So big, she couldn't even confess it to her best friend. Liz wondered if Maria had even confessed it to *herself*.

"Hey, I'm still a junior," Maria answered. "I have time. I'm not an old woman like you."

"Ha. Ha, ha," Liz muttered. She pushed her way out the big double doors leading to the main hallway.

"You know I'm right," Maria pressed. "If you keep going this way, you'll end up at your own senior prom with a just-friends guy."

That *was* a depressing thought. Liz still remembered back when she and Maria were eight years old. Every time they had a sleep over they would haul out the Barbie and Ken dolls and dress them up in their formal wear. Then they were off to the prom.

At one of those sleep overs Liz had called her papa and asked him if she could stay up until midnight on prom night. She hadn't thought there was anything silly about asking permission ten years in advance. He'd pretended to think it over very seriously, then said yes.

"And what about *after* high school?" Maria pressed. "What about college? What about the whole endless rest of your life? Are you going to spend all those years thinking about Max?"

Liz's stomach lurched. Maria had a point. She was starting to feel like she had some kind of obsessive-compulsive disorder, one where she had to think of Max sixty times a minute.

Maria grabbed her elbow. "You want a good place to start," Maria whispered. "A training-wheels guy?

44

Look over there." Maria gave her chin a jerk toward the far end of the hall.

Liz glanced over and saw Jerry Cifarelli standing in front of his locker. Jerry was one of those guys who seemed like an extra in the movie of high school. Always in the background. Sort of cute. Sort of smart. Sort of athletic. Sort of . . . *sort of* in every way, just not outstanding in even one area.

"Go on," Maria urged. "He's had a thing for you since you beat him out of the finals for the science fair when you were freshmen."

"First year," Liz corrected automatically. "Fresh*men* is a sexist term." She took another quick look at Jerry.

"At least go talk to him," Maria urged.

Max had made it totally clear that he wasn't going to let her get too close. She could either cry herself a river or move on.

"Okay. Time to move on," she muttered. She smiled at Maria. "I'll call you later."

A huge grin broke across Maria's face. "You better. I want to hear every word."

Liz felt calm as she walked toward Jerry. Totally calm. Calm in a way she never felt around Max. Not that she felt nervous around Max, exactly. Being around Max made her feel like she'd just taken a shower with a loofah sponge—all tingly and alive.

I sound like a bad commercial, Liz thought. Use loofah sponges and feel like you're in love.

In love. That was the whole problem. She was in love with Max. And that made every other guy seem *sort of*.

Too bad, Liz told herself. You're not getting out of this.

She tapped Jerry on the shoulder. "That pop quiz in bio was killer. I can't believe either of us is still standing."

"Yeah," Jerry agreed. "I stayed up till three, studying for a French test. I barely got through that, then—*bam, pop quiz.*"

"My friend Maria always tells me to drink a peach smoothie after monster days. She says that peaches are antitoxins. Or that the smell has a soothing effect. I can't remember which."

Okay, that was a nice, not too obvious hint, Liz thought. But did the boy get it?

Jerry heaved his backpack over his shoulder. "You, uh, want to go get one?" he asked.

"Sure," Liz said. "There's a place at the mall."

Jerry grinned. "Let's go."

Maria would be so proud, Liz thought as she followed him out into the parking lot.

"I'm right over there." Jerry pointed to a bright yellow Beetle, which was parked right next to Max's Jeep.

Just a little hello from the gods of irony, Liz thought. She forced herself to look over at the Jeep. She found Max staring back at her. The second her eyes met his, he dropped his gaze. But not before she saw the hurt expression.

Poor Max. She felt like running over to him and apologizing. But he'd had his chance. He could have had her in a heartbeat—and he knew it. It was his decision to push her away.

Now he'd have to live with it. They both would.

"Kevin, are you home?" Maria called.

Her little brother didn't answer. She didn't bother calling for her mom. Her mom was never home anymore. She was either at work or out on some date. Someday, maybe when she was about thirty-five, Maria would get used to the idea of her mom dating. And maybe when she was fifty, she'd get used to the idea that her parents were divorced.

Maria wandered into her room and spotted a folded piece of paper on her bed. She sat down and smoothed out the note. It said:

> *Dear Maria,*
> *I'm going out to dinner with friends after work. I borrowed your black sweater. Isn't it fun that we can wear the same size? Would you be an angel and make spaghetti for you and K? Thanks a trillion.*
>
> > *Love,*
> > *Mom*

Her black sweater. Her accidentally shrunk, so-tight-she-only-wore-it-around-the-house black sweater.

Her midriff-baring black sweater. Sorry, but Maria didn't buy the whole dinner-with-friends line. That sweater wasn't what you wore for something like that. Her mom was obviously going out with one particular *male* friend.

I'm never wearing that sweater again, Maria thought. No, not even. I'm going to start using that sweater as a dust rag. I can't believe she would wear that on a date. She shouldn't even be *going* on dates!

She decided she needed a shot of cedar. Cedar was the most calming scent. Maria grabbed her backpack and rooted around inside. She knew she'd brought a vial of cedar oil to school so she could take a whiff right before her oral report in English.

Maria's fingers closed around a tube, and she pulled it out. Nope, just a lipstick. It wasn't even hers. It was superdark, one of those plum shades. She loved the color, but it didn't work on her. Her face was all pale, and she had this light hair, so when she wore that color, she felt like a walking mouth, as if that was the only thing people saw when they looked at her.

It must be Liz's, Maria decided. Liz could definitely carry the color off. She was so dramatic looking, anyway, with her long black hair and dark eyes and those awesome cheekbones.

I wonder how it's going with Liz and Jerry? she thought. She felt something slither under her calf. What was that? She jerked her leg back. She didn't see anything.

Maria stood up and grabbed her bedspread in

both hands. She whipped it off and stared down at her bed. Her flowered sheets were dissolving into a mass of colored dots. No, not just the sheets, the whole *bed*. The whole bed was turning into a whirling mass of colored dots.

This isn't happening. This isn't happening, Maria thought. She squeezed her eyes shut. She would count to three and open her eyes. When she opened her eyes, everything would be back to normal. Everything. Would. Be. Back. To. Normal. It had to be.

One. Two. Three. Maria opened her eyes. Her whole room was a swirl of colored dots. No walls, no furniture, no nothing. Just dots. They whirled around her in a tornado of color, spinning faster and faster.

Maria's stomach lurched. A wave of dizziness pounded through her. Then the dots began to slow down. They clumped together, forming a polished floor under her feet, forming a shiny brass railing to her right, forming a row of stores to her left.

Forming the mall! She was standing on the upper deck of the mall.

She reached out and grabbed the railing that ran around the walkway. The metal felt cool under her fingers. Cool and solid. But how could it be?

Maria really needed that vial of cedar now. Don't panic, she told herself. You're okay. You're safe. You might have a mild case of insanity, but you're safe.

She took a deep breath and pushed herself away from the railing. A little girl rolled a doll stroller to-ward Maria. See, Maria thought. She looks perfectly normal. Just a happy little girl out with her doll.

The little girl kept coming toward Maria—and walked right through her. Did I die? Maria wondered. Did the thought of my mom dressed in my black sweater kill me? Am I some kind of ghost?

"Hey, I work as a waitress," a girl's voice said behind Maria. "So I know. He did not deserve a tip for pouring two peach smoothies."

That was Liz! Maria spun around and saw Liz and Jerry heading toward her.

"Liz, you have to help—" Maria knew her mouth was moving. She could feel it. But no sound was coming out.

The floor began to shift under her feet. She stumbled toward Liz. But she couldn't reach her. The mall was dissolving into colored dots.

Maria sank to her knees. She wrapped her arms around herself. The dots whipped past her. Then they started to clump. A few moments later they had reformed into her bedroom. And Maria was sitting on her own bed.

Maria's heart felt like it was trying to jerk its way out of her body. She pressed her hands over her chest—and felt something hard under her fingers. The ring.

Maria grabbed the chain and pulled the ring out and cupped it in her hands. It was glowing, spilling its purple-and-green radiance over her skin.

Maria brought the ring right in front of her eyes and kept her gaze locked on it as the eerie glow slowly faded. That was no trick of the light, she thought. And it wasn't my imagination, either.

Wait. Wait, she told herself. Before you start tweaking, try thinking like Liz again. In fact, maybe she should get the *actual* Liz to help her. Maria leaned over and grabbed her phone off her night table, then hit speed dial number one. Mrs. Ortecho answered on the second ring. She sounded kind of distracted, the way she always did when she was working. Maria didn't have to say who she was or anything. All she had to say was hello.

"Oh, Maria, hi," Mrs. Ortecho said. "Liz called and said she, uh, she was at the library and would be home in an hour or so." Maria heard some pans rattling around. "No, not at the library, the mall," Mrs. Ortecho corrected herself. Maria felt all the little hairs on her arms stand on end. "Want me to tell her to call you?"

"Sure. Thanks," Maria answered. She told Mrs. Ortecho good-bye and hung up. So Liz really *was* at the mall. Things were getting freakier by the second.

Calm down and pretend you're Liz. Think like a scientist, Maria told herself. Okay, what just happened obviously had something to do with the ring— or at least the stone in the ring. So what Liz would do is try and find out everything she could about the stone, get some hard facts.

Maria shoved herself to her feet and walked over to her bookshelf, taking each step slowly and carefully. She pulled down *The Encyclopedia of Stones and Crystals* and sat down at her desk with it. She flipped through the pages, searching for anything that looked like a possible match.

Not that one. Or that one. Maria turned another page, and a sidebar caught her eye. It was all about how some people believed stones and crystals could be used as a tool to enhance psychic abilities.

Psychic abilities. She'd been holding Liz's lipstick and wondering how things were going with her and Jerry—and then she *saw* Liz. That meant . . . that meant Maria had psychic abilities. Had the stone in the ring helped her tap into them?

Didn't some psychics use their *energy* to heal, too? If Maria was psychic, maybe she really had healed Sassafras the other day! Suddenly she felt filled with strength and energy. It was as if the ring's light was somehow burning deep inside her.

Whoa. And I'm the one who was sitting in Flying Pepperoni yesterday feeling like the ultimate girl next door, she thought. Boring with a big capital *B*. She'd been so afraid that some exotic alien girl was going to stroll into town and steal Michael away from her. Not that she exactly *had* him or anything.

But if she was right, there was nothing boring about her. She was *psychic*. That meant she had powers even Michael, Max, and Isabel didn't have.

Maria shook her head. She was getting way too excited way too fast. Probably what really happened was she came in her room, sat down on her bed, and dozed off for a few minutes. She always had the strangest, most vivid dreams when she slept during the day.

That was the most logical, scientific thing she'd thought yet. But Maria didn't quite believe it. A test— that's what she needed.

She could just use Liz's lipstick again. But it would be better—more scientific—if she did her test on someone different. That way she wouldn't have junk already in her head the way she would if she tried to *see* Liz again.

Kevin, Maria decided. There was plenty of her little brother's stuff all over the house. She rushed out of her room and stumbled over Kevin's baseball mitt. Yeah, you never had to go far to find something that belonged to slob boy Kevin.

Maria took the mitt back into her room and sat down on her bed. She dug her fingers into the leathery material. "I wonder what Kevin is doing right now," she whispered.

The bed rippled underneath her. Yes! It was working.

The room dissolved into colored dots and swooped around Maria. It's so beautiful, she thought. At least it is now that I'm not one hundred percent freaked out.

The dots began to clump, and Maria found herself standing in the parking lot of the minimart. Kevin and two of his buddies sat on the curb in front of the store.

"I can burp the Pledge of Allegiance," Kevin bragged. He grabbed his supersize soda and drained it in one long guzzling gulp. Maria could see the muscles in his throat working.

Kevin opened his mouth to burp, and the dots began to swirl. Good, Maria thought. Kevin was always making her listen to him burp stuff. She could stand to miss one of his little performances.

The dots clumped, and Maria was back in her room. She checked the ring—it was glowing again.

"Maarrriiia!" Kevin shouted outside her door. He knew better than to come in without permission.

"I'm not deaf, you know," she snapped. She swung herself off the bed and opened the door.

"Are you sure?" Kevin grumbled. "I called you about four thousand times."

"You called me *once*," she shot back. Somehow she always got into these stupid arguments with her little brother.

"Whatever," Kevin mumbled. "Aren't you supposed to be making dinner?"

"I don't know how you have any room for food with all that soda sloshing around inside you," she said.

Hold up, Maria thought. I just *saw* Kevin at the minimart. Even if he left right away, it would take him at least five minutes to ride his bike back here.

Kevin pulled an empty soda cup out of his backpack. "I only drank this much," he told her. "It's not even the biggest one they have."

The cup was exactly like the one she'd seen in her vision. This did not make sense. How could he be at the minimart ten seconds ago and here right now?

"Did you really call me a bunch of times before I answered?" she asked Kevin.

"Yeah. I was kind of hoping you were dead," he answered. "Except then I would have had to make my own spaghetti." He grinned at her over his shoulder as he headed down the hall to his room.

Maria leaned against the door frame and wrapped her arms around herself. It's like the other day, she thought. The way my clock jumped forward five minutes, right after I healed Sassy's paw.

She'd just thought the clock was messed up. But maybe—it seemed like two of the times she'd used her psychic powers, she'd lost a little time. Nothing much. Five minutes the other day. Maybe ten minutes after she'd *seen* Kevin.

Wait? Did I lose any time after I *saw* Liz in the mall? She had no idea. But she'd been alone in her room, so maybe she just hadn't noticed.

I wonder what happens to me during the missing time? It was kind of a creepy thing to think about. It can't be anything too bad, she told herself. I feel fine. Better than fine.

A slow smile spread across her face. I am definitely psychic, she thought. And that means I am most definitely *not* just your basic, ordinary human chick.

The Major stepped into Alex's doorway. "What's going on with the ROTC?"

Alex's dad was obsessed with having Alex coordinate starting up an ROTC program at school. He wouldn't be happy until every kid in Roswell spent every free moment doing push-ups and learning how to clean rifles or something. Alex wasn't exactly sure what you actually did in the ROTC. His dad had given him a ton of material on the program, and Alex had dutifully filed it away—in the circular file.

Of course he stuck it in a paper bag before he put it in the garbage. Alex didn't want to see the kind of meltdown his dad would have if he found the ROTC info in the trash.

"The Royal Orangutan Telepathic Committee?" Alex asked, keeping his voice all innocent.

"Time is a precious commodity," his dad answered. "When you waste my time, it's like stealing my wallet."

Alex sighed. The gods must have gotten a phone call or something right when they were about to give the Major a sense of humor. Either that or it was surgically removed when he joined the military.

Alex knew his dad. If he pushed his father too hard, the guy would suddenly remember that the garage needed cleaning or that the dog poop needed to be scooped up from the backyard. But Alex wanted every step of getting the ROTC running to be hard for his dad. He wanted to make his dad wish that he'd never come up with the idea in the first place. Although Alex knew that no matter what he did, eventually there would be an ROTC program at school. And he'd probably be in it.

"Alex, telephone," his mom called from the kitchen.

A distraction! Yes. "I'll give you an update later," Alex said, then bolted to the kitchen. He grabbed the phone from his mom. "I don't care who this is— you're my very best friend."

"Um, thanks."

Isabel. Her voice sounded funny, kind of cracked

and husky. Which made total sense. She hadn't been using her voice for much lately. Alex had gone to visit her every day for the last three days and spent the whole time basically talking to himself outside her door. Yesterday he had gotten so desperate he actually told her how he'd been terrified of Big Bird when he was two.

"How're you doing?" he asked. He was totally blown away that she'd called him.

"Okay . . . I guess. Actually, I wanted to ask you a favor. Like you haven't done enough for me already," she said.

Alex didn't like the tone in her voice. It was timid. So not Isabel. Yeah, she could be a pain in the butt when she got all arrogant, like she was the hottest thing ever and he should be grateful for a moment in her presence. But he hated hearing her sound so beaten down.

"You got it," he answered.

Isabel gave a half laugh. "Don't you even want to know what it is?" she asked.

"Hey, the way I see it, you've got me where you want me," he told her. "If I don't do what you want, you could tell everyone about, you know, the bird. I'd be listening to all my so-called friends sing the *Sesame Street* theme song for the rest of my pitiful life."

Isabel gave a real laugh that time. "My mom is absolutely refusing to let me stay home from school tomorrow. At least unless I agree to go to the doctor. So I was wondering if you could pick me up on your way," she said.

Alex didn't bother asking why she couldn't just ride with Max. He didn't care. "I'll be there," he promised.

"Great," she said.

So was the conversation over? Did she want him to talk more? Or would she just be like, "I call to ask him one thing and he doesn't let me off the phone"?

"So, uh, I'll see you in the morning," Isabel said.

She didn't say it in that way that made it clear it was time to say good-bye and hang up. He got the feeling she wasn't quite done. Like there was something else she wanted to say.

"Thank you for choosing Alex's Taxi Service," he joked. "Do you want to get to school early or anything? Or—"

"Alex, I don't know how to say this. But I've got to say it. Max says I'm really bad at it. But I have to do it, anyway," she blurted.

"Um, I have no idea what you're talking about," Alex told her. He heard Isabel take a shaky breath. "I want to apologize. But it's hard to know where to start. If I start back at that night we went miniature golfing, we'll be on the phone forever."

Alex remembered that night. He remembered the way Isabel looked him right in the eye, told him she knew exactly what she wanted, and kissed him. She then proceeded to basically forget he was alive because the next day she met Nikolas.

"Let me just give you the highlights," Isabel continued. "I'm really sorry for the way I acted when I was with Nikolas. Even after he hurt you, I still thought . . .

I don't know what I thought. I guess I wasn't thinking, at least not about anyone but myself."

"Isabel, you don't have—"

"Please just let me finish, okay?" she interrupted. "I was having so much fun that I didn't want to hear you telling me that I was putting myself—and everybody else—in danger. I should have listened to you. If I had, maybe . . ."

He could hear her fighting not to cry. But he didn't say anything this time. He figured it was better to let her get it out. "Anyway, I'm sorry. Especially for going off on you and saying you were just jealous of Nikolas. I know you were really trying to protect me," she said. "I—I have to go, okay? I'll see you tomorrow."

She hung up before he could accept her apology or say good-bye. Maybe that was a good thing. This way he didn't have to decide if he should tell her the truth. Yes, he told her to stay away from Nikolas because he was sure the guy was going to end up getting Isabel hurt.

But that didn't mean Isabel was wrong about Alex being jealous of Nikolas. Because he was. Pathologically jealous.

Alex reached into his pocket and pulled out a strip of photos that he'd found at a booth in the mall. He and the others had been trying to find Isabel and Nikolas before Valenti found *them*. Instead he'd come across these pictures of Isabel and Nikolas in the middle of a way too uninhibited make-out session.

He knew he should throw the pictures away. Especially the one where Nikolas was holding a sign that said, *Hi, Alex*. But he kept carrying them around with him.

Just looking at the pictures set off an explosion of jealousy inside him, which was so totally pathetic. How could he be jealous of a dead guy?

Alex gave a growl of frustration and threw the photos in the kitchen sink. He grabbed a box of matches from the junk drawer and set the pictures on fire.

If only he could burn Isabel's memory of Nikolas.

5

Isabel grabbed her lunch out of her locker and hurried down the hall, head lowered, eyes focused on her feet. All she wanted to do was get out to the quad. Alex would be there. And Max, Michael, Liz, and Maria.

She could feel people staring at her as she scurried along. She used to like being looked at. But not anymore. Now people were looking at her and whispering about Nikolas. She kept hearing his name—Nikolas, Nikolas, Nikolas. Everyone was gossiping about him . . . and her. Wondering what really happened to him. Trying to guess what the fight he and Isabel had the night he disappeared was about—somehow everyone had heard that lie she told Valenti.

"I bet Isabel killed Nikolas because he was going out with Stacey Scheinin on the side," Isabel heard someone whisper. Then she heard a burst of laughter. She smelled a whiff of gunpowder. Oh, God, no. It was starting again. The image of Nikolas falling to the floor, his eyes wide open and staring.

Isabel shoved her way out the main doors and ran around to the quad. She forced her eyes up and saw

Alex, Max, Liz, Maria, and Michael settled in their usual lunchtime spot. The smell of the gunpowder started to fade.

"Hey, Isabel. I heard you're in the market for some new man meat," a guy shouted. "I'm grade-A prime."

Isabel recognized the voice and the attitude. Usually she would have found a way to reduce Kyle Valenti to a writhing puddle of humiliation. But today all she wanted to do was get across the quad to her friends.

Just a few more steps, she told herself. Then she squeezed into the circle next to Alex. Some of the tightness in her chest relaxed, and she could breathe a little more easily.

"Do you want me to go beat up Kyle for you?" Liz asked. "I'd enjoy it, really."

"It's okay," Isabel mumbled. "But thanks." Liz was being so totally incredible. She'd called Isabel every night that Isabel had been out of school, and she and Maria had stopped by one morning with muffins and juice and a ton of magazines.

Neither one of them had even gotten close to saying, "I told you so, I told you Nikolas was going to put us all in danger." Neither one of them had given the slightest hint they were relieved that Nikolas was . . . was . . . Isabel shivered. Michael pulled off his jacket and tossed it to her. Typical Michael. Always there for her, without making a big deal out of it.

They had all been there for her—Michael, Liz, Maria. Plus Alex, her human tranquilizer, sitting outside her door hour after hour, talking until he was hoarse. And Max, in total big-brother mode, bossing her around, making sure she at least got out of bed every day.

"What is DuPris doing here?" Alex asked. "Don't they have laws about strange men wandering around talking to us children?"

Isabel glanced over her shoulder. Yeah, there was town wack job Elsevan DuPris. He strolled their way, twirling his walking stick between his palms, then veered off to talk to a group of kids over by the big oak tree.

Almost everyone in Roswell read DuPris's paper, the *Astral Projector*. But what DuPris didn't seem to realize was that they read it because the stories were hilarious. Isabel always loved it when he did one of his special reports on bloodsucking alien babies.

"If he offers you candy—run," Liz advised.

"I don't like the way he always *happens* to end up talking to us," Max said.

"Cheese it. Here he comes," Alex said.

Maria giggled. "Did you actually just say cheese it?"

"That I did," Alex answered. "That's my latest list. Food-related expressions. Which you would know if you cared enough to check out my web site."

"Hello, young people," DuPris called as he ambled up to them. "You look like some of the brightest and best of your classmates."

Michael smirked. "Why, aren't you just as sweet as pie," he drawled, imitating DuPris's fakeoid southern accent.

Isabel choked back a laugh. This was the good

part about rejoining the outside world. Here she was just a normal girl hanging out with her friends in the quad, a group in the middle of all the other groups. There was nothing more normal than that.

"I'm doing an opinion poll for my little paper," DuPris told them. "If you would be so kind, I'd like you to answer me this question. If you were an alien and you went to our lovely shopping mall, what would you buy?"

The mall. Why is he asking about the mall? Isabel thought. Her heart gave a hard double-fast beat. Could Valenti have told him he shot an alien there? Or does he have some other source? Does he know I was there, too? Does he know the truth about me?

Isabel shifted her weight so her arm grazed Alex's. She needed to feel the warmth of his body.

"It would have to be . . . a Crock-Pot," Alex said.

"Absolutely," Michael jumped in.

"If I were an alien, I'd find a Crock-Pot pretty much irresistible," Max agreed.

"They're so convenient," Liz added.

"And there's so little cleanup time," Maria chimed in.

DuPris raised one eyebrow as he turned to Isabel. "And you, young lady, do you agree with your witty friends?"

She cleared her throat. "Crock-Pot gets my vote. Uh-huh."

"Why, I thank you, and I hope to see you all again soon." DuPris gave them a little wave and set off.

"Do you think he knows?" Isabel asked the second he was out of earshot.

"He might know *something* happened at the mall," Max said slowly. "One of the UFO heads might have reported a strange light. When Ray used his power to trap Valenti inside, it was almost blinding."

"That makes sense," Liz agreed.

"You don't think Valenti told him the truth?" Isabel asked.

"No way. Valenti would probably just kill DuPris if he found out the truth. I don't think the Project Clean Slate boys want anybody in their business," Alex said.

He was right. Of course he was right. Isabel really, really had to get a grip.

"What are you guys doing after school?" Isabel said in a rush, trying to force her mind away from the horrible movie that played and replayed in her mind. "Maybe we could go to the frozen yogurt place or something."

"Michael and I are meeting Ray at the cave," Max answered. "He's going to show us some stuff that we can do with our power. We can do so much more than we ever thought."

"What? But using powers could attract Valenti's attention," Isabel cried. "I'm never using mine again— for anything. You guys have to promise me you won't, either. Promise me!"

"Isabel, take it easy," Max said.

"No!" she shot back. "If Nikolas and I hadn't used our powers, Valenti never would have come after us." Isabel felt hot tears flood her eyes. She wiped them away with the back of her hand. "Nikolas would still be alive and we wouldn't have to be afraid," she forced herself to continue. "So you can't use your powers at all. Ever. We just have to act like regular humans."

"Ray says there are ways to cloak power use," Michael said.

"No. Don't even try to convince me," Isabel answered.

"But your power is an incredible gift, Isabel. If Ray can teach you how to use it safely—," Maria began.

"Drop it!" Isabel snapped. "You have no idea what you're talking about. You don't know what it's like to have these powers!"

Maria quickly looked away, her cheeks flushing.

Isabel sighed. "I'm sorry, Maria. I didn't mean to yell at you. I just . . . I wish I could just be normal like you."

"Iz . . . ," Michael said.

The bell rang, cutting him off. Isabel jumped to her feet.

"Look, you guys go see Ray without me if you need to," she said. "I have no desire to spend hours at the cave, listening to some old guy blabber. I have to get to class." Yeah, class. That was a good normal-human-girl thing to do. "Are you coming, Maria?"

"Sure." Maria didn't meet Isabel's eyes. Uh-oh, Isabel thought. Maybe I really insulted her with that you-have-no-idea-what-it's-like comment. Still, even if Maria was mad at her, it was better than walking to class alone.

She followed Maria down the hall to English, slid into her seat, and pulled out her copy of *Julius Caesar*.

They'd been studying the play for weeks. No more thinking of Nikolas. All she had to do now was listen to the teacher.

Ms. Markham made her way to the front of the class. Isabel noticed that she had a piece of what looked like tuna salad on the front of her shirt. The woman should wear a bib.

"Time to get started," Ms. Markham said. "We left off at Portia's speech, so begin, Portia."

Nobody began to read. Isabel glanced around the room. She didn't see anybody looking for their book or trying to find the right page or anything.

"Same roles as yesterday," Ms. Markham said. "Who is our Portia?"

"It was Maria," Arlene Bluth called.

"All right, Maria," Ms. Markham called. "No more time to get in character. We have a lot of pages to cover."

Maria didn't begin to read. Isabel twisted around in her seat and stared down the row.

Something was wrong. Maria held the play in her hands. But she was gazing at it as if she'd forgotten what it was.

"Maria?" Ms. Markham prodded.

"Uh, Maria wasn't feeling that well at lunch," Isabel said quickly, standing up. "I'll take her to the nurse."

Isabel didn't wait for Ms. Markham to answer. She grabbed Maria's arm and led her out of the classroom and down the hall to the bathroom.

"What's going on?" Isabel demanded. "Are you okay?"

Maria didn't answer. She stared straight ahead, her eyes blank.

Isabel's heart began to slam against her ribs. What was going on? Maria was fine a couple of minutes ago when they were walking to class. She was mad, but she was *fine*.

"Maria," Isabel shouted. Her voice echoed off the bathroom's tile walls. But the sound got no response from Maria.

Isabel wanted to run and get Alex, or Max or Michael or Liz. But she didn't want to leave Maria alone. You can deal with this, she told herself. Maria needs you.

She pulled in a deep, shuddering breath, then reached out and rested her fingers on the side of Maria's neck. Yes, she could feel a pulse. It was faint and sort of erratic, but it was there.

Isabel bit her lip. Should I connect with her? she wondered. Maybe then I could find out what's wrong. Isabel reached for Maria again but hesitated. I can't use my powers, her mind screamed. Valenti will find me and kill me!

Isabel took Maria by the shoulders and gave her a little shake. "Maria, come on! Snap out of it!"

Maria didn't even blink.

"Maria, you are scaring the hell out of me," Isabel cried. She didn't want to use her healing powers. She just couldn't.

She shook Maria harder, shook her until her head was jerking back and forth.

"What are you doing?" Maria demanded.

68

"You talked!" Isabel stared at her. Maria's blue eyes had lost that creepy blank look.

"Of course I talked. You were practically shaking my head off," Maria answered.

"Are you okay?" Isabel demanded. "Should I go get someone?"

"I'm okay," she answered. "But what are we doing in here?"

Isabel felt her spine turn to ice. "Don't you remember?" she asked. "You totally spaced in English."

"Uh-uh." Maria shook her head. "I, um, I knew I shouldn't have eaten that candy bar Alex gave me. Sugar totally messes me up." She grabbed Isabel by the arm. "Come on, we better get back to class."

"Maria, what's going on?" Isabel pressed.

"Nothing. Nothing, I'm fine," Maria insisted. "Let's go."

Frowning, Isabel followed her out into the hall. Maria sounded completely fine. But there was no way a little sugar could have gotten that reaction.

No possible way.

Max sat on the floor of the cave and leaned against the cool limestone wall behind him. He felt like he'd pulled a muscle in his brain, a muscle he hadn't even realized was there. Ray had been trying to teach them how to do that time-freezing thing he'd done at the mall. But neither Max nor Michael had gotten close to getting it right.

"Using your brain is more tiring—and more difficult—than using your body," Ray said. He lowered himself onto a big rock across from Max. Michael didn't waste any time sitting. He stretched out flat on his back on the floor.

"Wait. Did you just read my mind again?" Max demanded. The stuff Ray could do was amazing. Thinking about it made Max's head hurt even more.

"Just a little," Ray answered.

He must have caught the look of panic and embarrassment on Max's face—or else read Max's mind *again*—because he laughed. "Don't worry, when I do it, I don't go too deep. I don't want to bump up against anything too personal. You never know what you're going to find in a teen's head."

Ray pulled a Lime Warp out of his backpack. He

popped the top of the drink. "Want one?" he asked.

"That stuff tastes like goat piss," Michael complained. But he took a Lime Warp, anyway, then flopped back down next to Max.

"You know this for a fact?" Max asked. He grabbed a can from Ray. "You've actually tasted goat piss and can make an accurate comparison?"

"There are times you sound way too much like that science guy on TV," Michael said. "You know—the walking, talking dork?" He took a slug of his drink, then studied the can. "I still can't believe this is what we really look like. No offense, Ray."

Max glanced at the little dancing alien on the can. It did have the same small body, big head, and huge, almond-shaped, pupil-less eyes as everyone Ray had shown them on the spaceship.

"No, you've got it wrong. Well, sort of," Ray told Michael. "This form"—he pointed to the drawing on the Lime Warp can—"isn't any more our true appearance than this one." He gestured to his human body.

Max pressed his soda can against his pounding head. Ray had kept the drinks icy cold by slowing down the movement of the molecules. Max could have done that, too—if he'd thought of it—but it would have taken total concentration. Ray did it as easily as popping the top of the cans.

"I'm confused," Max admitted. "Maybe it's because I still have brain strain, but I don't get it."

"It's not all that complicated," Ray answered. "Here's the short version. Our bodies are highly adaptable. They adjust to whatever environment

71

we're in. That means we can travel to any planet without the elaborate space suits humans use because our bodies automatically configure themselves for optimal functioning. Even on our own planet our bodies change, depending on factors like the climate."

"Can I just say, *huh?*" Michael asked.

"I sort of get it," Max said. "Earth is an environment with an oxygen-rich atmosphere. So our bodies configured themselves to breathe oxygen. Is that what you mean?"

"Ding, ding, ding. Give the boy a prize," Ray called out. "That's it exactly. What you just described is one of the thousands of ways our bodies adapt."

"Okay, I know I haven't read every science book in the world, like Max has, but I do know human bodies aren't the best choice for adapting to life in the desert," Michael said. "How come we don't look more like scorpions or cacti or something?"

"The answer is that our bodies don't just adapt to the physical environment," Ray said. "They adapt to the social environment, too. Humans are the species that dominates the planet, so our adaptation system gave us bodies to match theirs."

"So how do these guys fit in?" Max held up the Lime Warp can.

"Another adaptation, this time to life in space. The density of the small bodies protects their internal systems from the effects of rapid space travel. And the small bodies take up less space on board, freeing up room for more important items," Ray said.

"Cool," Michael said.

"Very cool," Max agreed. "Could you show us some hologram pictures, or whatever you call them, of some of the *adaptations* we have at home?"

"Home. I don't understand why you're calling it home," Ray said. *"This* is your home. Earth. It was a mistake for me to tell you anything about . . . that other place. I try to think of it as a dream, a beautiful dream. But not something real, not something I can ever go back to. This is my home now, too."

He sounded so sad suddenly, not his usual joking self. Max wondered how he would feel if he had to make a life on another planet, knowing he'd never see his parents or Liz or anyone else he cared about again. He didn't know if he'd cope as well as Ray seemed to have.

Ray stood up. "Let's get out of here."

"So that's it. You're not answering any more questions? You're just deciding for us that we shouldn't know anything about where we come from?" Michael demanded.

Ray looked directly at Michael. "I'm not going to encourage you to spend your lives wishing you were someplace else," he said. "Your lives are here. Get on with them."

"Thanks for nothing," Michael muttered.

Ray turned to Max. "I know it must seem that I'm being incredibly harsh. But trust me, living one place when your heart and mind are always somewhere else is guaranteed to make you miserable."

Max didn't want to push Ray. It was pretty clear that he was protecting himself as much as he was Max and Michael. But there was one thing he had to know.

"Can you just tell—," Max said.

"Max, I've made up my mind," Ray interrupted.

"This is important," Max insisted. "I just want to know if there's anything you can teach me that will help protect us from Valenti."

Ray sighed. "I guess that is something you actually do need to know. We can do some more work freezing time inside a particular location. But that's not something you can do often. I won't be able to do it again myself for at least a month—it takes too much energy."

"Is there anything else?" Max asked. He wanted to be prepared, no, he *needed* to be prepared if he had to go up against Valenti again. It's not like Ray would always be able to come to the rescue.

"Lay low. That's what got me through the last fifty-something years," Ray answered.

"That's it? Lay low?" Michael demanded.

"Well, there is a little trick I use sometimes," Ray admitted. "Watch this."

"Watch what?" Max asked. Then he saw it. Ray's face was *moving*. His hair was growing and darkening. His body was shrinking and changing shape.

He looked like . . . Liz. Ray looked like Liz.

"Aaaah." Michael gave a high, comical shriek.

"We can also give ourselves little makeovers whenever we want to change our appearance," Ray said. He even sounded like Liz. "I gave myself one after the crash. I didn't feel like being the scientist the people in Roswell knew anymore."

"You're giving me the creeps," Max said. He could

hardly stand to look at Ray. There were just way too many things he didn't want to think about. Like the fact that Ray had grown a set of breasts . . . *Liz's* breasts.

"Okay, okay." Ray's voice got deeper as he took back his usual form.

"You even sounded like her," Max mumbled.

"It's all in the vocal cords," Ray said. "Did you hear about that Elvis sighting at a little taco stand in El Paso?" he asked.

Max shook his head.

"Me," Ray bragged. He sounded totally proud of himself.

Max cracked up. He knew Ray was an Elvis fan, but this was pretty out there.

"Doing my part to keep the King alive," Ray said. "Thank you very much," he added in a decent Elvis mumble.

"You've got to show us how to do that," Max said.

"Why didn't you say yes when Jerry asked you to go to UFOnics with him?" Maria demanded as soon as Liz stepped back behind the Crashdown Café's counter.

Liz snorted. "I knew you heard the whole conversation. You only wiped down the booth next to Jerry's three times."

"Four," Maria admitted. "But if I *don't* watch you every second, you'll slide back into daydreaming about Max, ignore all other guys, and end up a dried-up old woman with sixteen yapping Pomeranians."

"If you don't stop, you're going to end up with this sponge down your throat," Liz threatened. She held up the sponge and advanced on Maria.

Maria backed away. "Did I mention that you'd be so pathetic that all the Poms would be named Max? Or Maxine? Or Maximilian? Or Maxi? Or—"

"Did I mention that I used this sponge to wipe off Mr. Orndorff's table?" Liz asked.

"The spitter?" Maria squealed. "Okay, I'll stop, I'll stop. But I still want to know why you told Jerry you'd let him know tomorrow instead of saying yes."

"It's the dancing thing," Liz said. "If he'd asked me to go somewhere besides UFOnics, I'd probably have said yes."

"But you're a great dancer," Maria protested.

"It's not the dancing part of the dancing," Liz explained. "It's the *touching* part of the dancing."

"The touching thing is going to come up, dancing or not," Maria said. "Say he asked you to a movie. Major touching potential sitting in the dark. Even if he asked you bowling, at some point he'd take you home, and then the touching issue would be right there."

"I guess." Liz didn't sound convinced.

The opening bars of the *Close Encounters* theme filled the café. Maria glanced over to see Liz's dad come in, whistling a Grateful Dead song.

Maria swung up the hinged section of the counter for Mr. Ortecho. "I won't dock you this time, but if you're late again, you won't be so lucky," she teased.

"Oh, Ms. DeLuca, I'm sorry. Don't be mad," Mr.

Ortecho cried in a breathy voice. "There was a sale on this suit that I've had my eye on for, like, months, and I had to get it on my way to work or it would have been gone. Here, just smell this. It will make you feel better."

Maria giggled. "I don't sound like that," she protested.

"You sound exactly like that," Liz said. She grabbed the coffeepot and headed over to a table where two very serious UFologists were studying a map of the crash site.

Maria yawned and rested her elbows on the counter. She was exhausted. Ever since school today she'd felt weird. No matter how hard she tried, she couldn't stop thinking about that blackout in English class.

Maybe I should have told Isabel the truth, she thought. But it was Isabel's first day back at school, and she had enough to deal with. Someday soon I'll tell them all about my psychic abilities, Maria thought. As soon as I figure out how to control my powers, then I'll give everyone a big demonstration.

But she couldn't control them. Today in class, for instance, Maria had been sitting at her desk, waiting for Ms. Markham to show up. She started running her fingers across one of the names that someone had carved into her desk, wondering how long the name had been there and what the guy who carved it was doing now.

She hadn't been trying to *see* the guy. But the dots had started to swirl, and a few seconds later she'd been standing in a used-car lot watching a paunchy guy try to sell a Honda to a twenty-something woman in a business suit. The dots had swirled again, and the classroom had re-formed.

The next thing she remembered was Isabel shaking her, obviously one second away from a total meltdown. Maria knew using her power had caused her to lose another few minutes, but it didn't seem like a good time to explain that to Isabel. Especially after the way Isabel had snapped at her at lunchtime.

Maria knew psychic powers weren't the same as alien powers, but Isabel seemed ready to yell at anyone who even *talked* about using powers.

"Earth to Maria!" Liz's voice broke into her thoughts.

Maria narrowed her eyes at her best friend. "So," she said. "UFOnics with Jerry?"

Liz chewed her lip. "I don't know. . . ."

Maria shook her head sadly. "I have two words to say to you—"

"Pomeranian better not be one of them," Liz warned.

"Just friends," Maria said. She didn't mean to be harsh, but sometimes Liz really needed a push. "You know I'm right," she added. "Max already made this decision for you."

Liz sighed. "Okay. Okay, okay, okay," she said. "I'll go tell Jerry."

"We have the place to ourselves," Isabel announced as she unlocked her front door. "Max is at work, and so are my parents." She led the way into the living room.

Alex wondered if girls had any idea what effect *words* could have on a guy. Words like "we have the place to ourselves." Six basic words, not one of them sexual or anything. But whoa. They sent a shock wave through Alex's body.

She just meant it as your basic informational statement, he told himself. Like "we have some soda in the fridge" or "we get HBO." It wasn't some kind of invitation.

He sat down on the couch. Isabel sat next to him—so close, he could feel the heat of her body.

Or wait, he thought. Was I wrong? Was it a total girl-speak invitation? A notch down from something like "my bed has a very firm mattress"?

Because if it *was* an invitation, then he should accept. It was the polite thing to do.

Stop this. Right now, Alex ordered himself. Try to regrow a brain. Of course it's not an invitation, you moron. She saw the guy she loved get killed about two seconds ago.

Alex took a deep breath—and the scent of Isabel's spicy citrus perfume filled his nose. Oh, great. Would it look totally ridiculous if he got up and moved to that chair across from the couch? Because that would make things a lot easier.

Or maybe they could go upstairs. She could lock herself in her room, and he could sit outside the door and talk. He was really good at that.

"Do you want to watch TV?" Isabel asked.

No hidden meaning in those six words at least. "Sure," Alex said.

Isabel handed him the remote, a surprising move from her. Not that she was totally selfish. Not totally. But she did like things her own way—even little things like what TV show to watch—and she pretty much expected people to cooperate.

Alex flipped on the TV and started channel surfing. Isabel moved a little closer to him, making actual skin-to-skin contact between his arm and her arm. His brothers would laugh themselves sick if they could see their little brother getting all excited by touching some girl's *arm*.

But Isabel . . . she could turn him inside out with one look from those killer blue eyes. It had been that way since the first day he transferred to Olsen High. He saw her in the hall. She ignored him.

"Is this okay?" Alex asked, stopping on one of the endless talk shows.

"Sure," she answered. "Do you want something to drink?"

Another safe six words. But it would be even safer

in here if he could get her away from him for a minute. Maybe when she was gone, he'd move over to the chair. That would be okay. Sort of casual.

And while he was over there, he'd remind himself a few hundred times that this was not a guy-girl event. This was a friend-friend event. Where one friend—that would be him—helped a beautiful, blond, perfectly bodied friend—that would be her— get through a really bad time. Maybe next time he did this, he'd bring Liz. Or Liz *and* Maria. He could use some chaperons.

Isabel stood up. He thought she would head into the kitchen. But she didn't. She just stood there, staring down at him. He stared back, trying to figure out what she was thinking from the expression on her face.

Then she was on his lap. He didn't know if he reached up and pulled her to him or if she flung herself into his arms. It didn't matter. She was there. And her lips were on his.

So maybe it really was an invitation, he thought. And then he couldn't think at all. He was totally caught up in the feel of her hands in his hair. Her breasts against his chest. Her tongue brushing his.

He was not going to survive this. He was going to combust. Burst into flames so hot, there would be nothing left of him but a pile of cinders.

He didn't care. All he cared about was getting even closer. He couldn't get close enough. Alex wrapped his hands around Isabel's waist and pulled her tighter against him. He thought he heard her give a little whimper of pleasure.

He reached up to stroke her cheek—and his fingers came away wet. His eyes snapped open. And the fire burning through him went out.

Isabel was crying. Tears streaked her face. Alex suddenly realized he could taste salt on his lips. Oh, God. She'd been crying her heart out, and he'd been so caught up in the feel of her mouth, of her body, he hadn't even noticed.

He was an idiot. A moron. Like that little whimper was Isabel getting all passionate because she was into the way Alex was touching her. Right.

"I'm sorry," Isabel mumbled, her voice husky.

"It's okay. It's fine." Alex wanted to jump up and run out of the house. But that's not what Isabel needed from him. She needed him to be there as a friend. She needed him to hold her as a friend.

Alex pulled Isabel's head down on his shoulder. He cradled her in his arms. "You should go ahead and cry. It's good to cry. My mom is always saying that. Try convincing a house full of guys that, though."

He kept talking, saying anything that sprang into his head, keeping his voice low and calm. Trying not to think about her arms around his neck, her body pressed against his.

"I'm so glad you're here," Isabel said, her voice muffled against his shirt.

Alex knew it wasn't true. He knew there was only one guy Isabel really wanted here with her. And it wasn't him.

*　　　*　　　*

"Dylan, do you know what the—" Michael stopped, censored himself. "Do you know what a kimbie is?" he yelled. He didn't know exactly where Dylan was, so Michael yelled loud enough that he could be heard anywhere in the entire house.

He hoped that little weasel Dylan hadn't snuck out. The Pascals had said he was supposed to be helping Michael with the baby-sitting. And he was going to be one very sorry junior high school rodent if he didn't answer Michael pretty fast.

Michael tried to spoon another bite of applesauce into the baby's mouth. Sarah, that was her name. After so many foster families it got a little hard to keep track.

Sarah let the applesauce slide into her mouth and spat it back out. Then she laughed. Michael actually had thought the move was kind of cute—the first time. Now that a jar of baby bananas, a jar of baby spinach, and half a jar of baby applesauce were decorating the kitchen, it was getting old. Very old.

"I want kimbie," Amanda screeched from the next room. Who knew a five-year-old girl who insisted on dressing up like a fairy princess every day could yell that loud? Maybe he should try telling her that fairy princesses had very, very soft voices.

"Dylan!" Michael roared. "Get in here now! If I have to come looking for you, it's not going to be pretty."

Dylan stuck his head into the kitchen, careful to stay out of Sarah's spitting range. "I'm doing my homework. This is my homework time according to the Pascals' Rascals rules."

Michael almost believed the kid was serious. Then he saw the little smirk pulling on Dylan's lips. "The Pascals aren't here right now," he shot back. "You're living under my rules. And I'm giving you a new homework assignment—find out what a kimbie is and give it to Amanda so she'll stop screaming her little head off. Then put her in her pajamas and put her to bed."

"How am I supposed to—," Dylan began.

"Just do it," Michael barked. Dylan disappeared.

I should tell the Pascals there are people you can hire to do this kind of thing, Michael thought. People called baby-sitters.

That gave him an idea. Maria seemed like the kind of girl who would get into baby-sitting. He reached for the phone and dialed. Maria answered on the second ring. He wasn't proud. He begged. And she said she'd come right over.

You can hold out for fifteen minutes until Maria gets here, he told himself. "And you, Sarah, you can get some food down your gullet in fifteen minutes," he muttered.

Michael used his sleeve to wipe some mushed banana off his forehead, then scooped up another spoonful of applesauce. Sarah giggled in anticipation. He tried to tune out the sound of Amanda's yelling as he brought the spoon up to Sarah's mouth. He ordered *himself* not to yell when the applesauce hit his forehead and started dripping into his eye.

When Maria walked through the door thirteen minutes later, there was one horrible moment when

Michael was sure she was going to turn around and walk right back out.

But she didn't. First she told Dylan to get some crayons and paper and have Amanda draw a picture of the kimbie. It worked. They still didn't know what it was she wanted, but she was at least quiet and happy.

Then she dragged Michael into the kitchen to deal with Sarah. "Did any food actually make it down her throat, you think?" Maria asked. She reached up and twisted her hair into a ponytail. The gesture pulled her shirt tight against her body—and Michael flashed on Maria's dream.

That happened way too much lately. Maria would do some completely normal thing, and Michael would get slammed by the memory of that dream. He should never have gone into it. What he saw had totally messed up his head, turning his thoughts about Maria from G—okay, sometimes PG—to NC-17.

Like at lunch yesterday, she insisted that he and Alex eat at least one green thing. He reached over to take a celery stick from her, his hand brushed hers, he noticed her skin felt really soft. And suddenly he was wondering how it would feel to have those smooth hands of hers touching him *everywhere*.

"If you have to think that hard, I'd say the answer is no," Maria said.

"Uh, yeah. Right," Michael answered.

"We should probably wait and see if she feels hungry a little later. She's too hyped to eat right now," Maria decided. "I'll give her a bath. That should help relax her a little." She grabbed a dish towel and tossed it to Michael. "You can give the kitchen a bath."

Michael was glad to have something to do that would take his eyes off Maria for a while—even though he could still hear her splashing around in the kitchen sink, talking to the baby.

Why did she have to look so sexy in that dream? Cute. That's how Maria should look. It's how she'd always looked before. He remembered how annoyed she'd gotten when he used the *cute* word to describe her. She thought the word *cute* should only be used when you talked about kittens or something. He thought the way she got all ruffled up about it was . . . cute.

That's how he wanted to think of Maria. He wished there was some way of going into his brain and cutting out the piece that held the memory of her dream. He wanted his Maria thoughts to be able to get a PG rating again.

He scrubbed the table so hard, it made his arms ache, refusing to allow himself even a glance at Maria. Then he moved on to Sarah's high chair, the kitchen cabinets, and the floor. Sarah had done some throwing before she got to the spitting. The girl had a good arm.

"Okay, she's done. Can you get me a towel and some clean clothes?" Maria asked.

"Dylan, get us a towel and some clean clothes for Sarah," Michael called. He decided it was okay to look at her now. She was talking to him. He couldn't stare at the floor like an idiot. Michael glanced over at her. Big mistake. Sarah had splashed water all over Maria and her shirt now had some *interesting* semitransparent spots. Michael locked his gaze on her face.

Maria raised her eyebrows. "I always wanted a little brother," Michael admitted. "You know, someone to get me stuff when I was too lazy to do it myself."

"Oh, that's horrible, isn't it, Sarah?" Maria leaned down and kissed the baby on the head.

Michael suddenly regretted not going for the towel and clothes himself. Because watching Maria kiss Sarah's head made him think about her kissing him. And that was completely sick.

Sarah splashed in the water, kicking her pudgy legs. Maria laughed and kissed her again. Michael wondered what it would be like if she did kiss him. And not on the top of his head, either—more like the way she'd kissed that guy in her dream.

Don't even go there, he ordered himself. It would be way too weird. She was the girl he felt protective of, the girl he liked to tease, the girl he liked to scare when they were watching old horror movies. Kissing Maria would be too much like kissing a little sister.

Dylan wandered into the kitchen and dropped the towel and clothes on the table. "A kimbie is a baseball mitt, if you want to know," he muttered. "She likes to sleep with it."

"Good going," Michael said.

Dylan nodded. He crossed to the fridge, opened it, poked around a little, and shut it. He pretended to be all interested in watching Maria dress the baby, which Michael knew he wasn't. He got himself a drink of water, drank it, and poured another one.

"Did you need something, Dylan?" Maria finally asked. She picked up Sarah and held the baby cradled against her chest.

Michael stared at Dylan. It was better than looking at Maria. He hoped in a couple more days, the memory of that dream would start to fade and things would get back to normal. He wanted to be able to hang out with her without having . . . thoughts.

"Um, there's this dance on tomorrow . . . ," Dylan said. He shifted his weight from foot to foot.

Michael tried to figure out what the problem was. "Are you afraid the Pascals won't give you permission to go?" he asked.

"No, they already said I could go. Mr. Pascal's going to drive me," Dylan answered. "But I don't know how to dance," he confessed in a rush.

Michael shot a glance at Maria and caught her trying not to smile. He tried not to smile back.

"Dancing's easy. We can teach you," Maria said. "I'll just go put the baby down. Dylan, show me where?"

I guess I better go pick out some CDs, Michael thought. He headed to his room—well, his and Dylan's room. He was serious when he told Maria he'd always wanted a little brother. And not only so he'd have someone who he could make wait on him—that was a bonus.

Getting ready to teach Dylan to dance was giving him this big-brother feeling, a little taste of what it could have been like. Although *his* brother wouldn't have been such a dweeb he *needed* to be taught how to dance when he was, like, thirteen years old. Michael would have made sure of that. If he had a little brother, he would have made sure the kid was able to handle himself.

Michael didn't know why he was bothering to think about this. He was never going to have a little brother. Or a big brother or a sister or parents.

"Michael, come on," Maria called from the living room. "I want to shake my groove thing."

He laughed. Maria could always do that. She could always make him laugh. And that's what he needed—especially when he was about to sink into a bunch of pathetic thoughts about not having a family. He grabbed a few CDs, then jerked open his middle dresser drawer and snagged a sweatshirt and hurried back to the living room.

"I thought you might be cold. You got all wet," he told Maria. He threw the sweatshirt to her, and she pulled it on. Good.

Michael popped one of the CDs into the player and cranked it.

Dylan instantly stiffened up. "So what do I do?" he asked.

"Whatever you want," Maria cried over the music. "That's the best thing about dancing." She twirled around the room, giving little hops, doing her happy dance.

Michael attempted to keep his thoughts in line by focusing on Dylan, who looked totally panicked. "Don't worry, not everybody dances like Maria," Michael said. "All you have to do is kind of shuffle your feet around."

"It's true," Maria said. "That's what Michael does. And there are usually a few girls desperate enough to dance with him."

Dylan laughed. Maria grabbed his hands and pulled him around the room a few times. Michael stepped back and watched. Maria was right about him. He was an okay dancer, but he never got into it the way she did. It's like the music took her over, from all those springy blond curls to—

Get a grip, Michael told himself. As soon as the song was over he killed the music. "You'll be fine," Michael told Dylan.

"But what about, you know, slow dancing?" Dylan asked.

"Even easier," Michael answered. "You don't even really have to shuffle your feet. You just kind of hold the girl and sway."

"But"—Dylan lowered his voice, sounding embarrassed—"but where . . . *where* are you supposed to hold her?"

Maria changed CDs and a slow song started up. She turned off the overhead light. "You can't slow dance when it's this bright," she said. She stepped up to Michael. "You can use me to demonstrate."

He didn't want to touch her right now. Not with all those thoughts about her wet shirt filling his brain. But he couldn't think of a way out of it.

"There are a couple of places your hands can go. I usually put mine here," Michael told Dylan. He positioned his hands in the curve of Maria's waist.

"A good choice," Maria said. "The girl might do

90

something like this." She linked her hands behind Michael's neck.

This felt . . . pretty nice. It didn't feel all wrong and awkward the way he thought it would.

"Is that how far away I should be?" Dylan asked. Any second Michael expected him to pull out some paper and start taking notes.

"Probably to start," Maria said. "But there are signals that a girl wouldn't mind being held a little closer. Like she might stare into your eyes."

Maria looked up at Michael. Man, her eyes were blue. And she always smelled so good.

Michael wondered what the deal was with her dream. *Was* there some guy out there she had a thing for, some guy she wanted to kiss? Or did she wake up the next morning going, "That was weird. I guess I shouldn't eat pineapple pizza before I go to bed."

"Or she might move her arms around your waist." Maria demonstrated on Michael, and it continued to feel good. He kept waiting for that wave of but-this-is-the-girl-who's-like-my-little-sister feeling to sweep over him. But it didn't come.

"That's a pretty clear signal she wants to be held closer," Maria said. "Of course, some guys, like Michael, are kind of slow. They miss the more subtle hints."

"I'm not missing any hints," Michael answered. He pulled her up against him and slid one of his hands up her back. She snuggled closer, resting her cheek against his chest. That little-sister feeling still didn't come.

"So that's it?" Dylan asked.

"That's it," Michael answered. He started to pull away, but Maria tightened her arms around him.

"There is the kissing thing," Maria said. She lifted her head and stared up at Michael again.

"The kissing thing?" Dylan repeated in horror.

"Yeah, sometimes during a slow dance people kiss," Maria said.

Michael's eyes drifted down to her lips. The color of them reminded him of raspberries. He wondered how they would taste.

But kissing was a whole different deal than dancing. Dancing was kind of a borderline. You could be friends and dance together. But if you started kissing, you crossed the border from being friends into . . . something else.

"I think you've learned enough for one night," Michael told Dylan.

Max glanced at the clock. Almost eight. Was Liz changing clothes right now, trying to decide what to wear to UFOnics, trying to figure out what Jerry Cifarelli would think was hot?

"What do you think of a display on the Hollow Earth Society?" Ray asked. "Maybe right over there, next to the one on the Elvis-alien connection." He jerked his chin, nodding toward the back wall of the UFO museum.

"I don't know what that is," Max admitted.

Maybe Liz and Jerry are already at UFOnics, dancing to some slow song, Max thought. Why had Maria told him that Liz was going out with Jerry tonight? If she wanted to torture him, why didn't she just pull out his fingernails or drip water on his forehead?

"And you call yourself an alien," Ray scolded. "Don't you know we've been colonizing the hollow center of the earth for hundreds of years?"

"Wait. *What?* When were you planning on telling us?" Max demanded. He understood that talking about their birth planet was painful for Ray. But if there was a whole group of aliens on *earth*, he should know about it.

Ray shook his head. "Max, Max, Max. You really should have told me you'd gone in for that lobotomy. I'd have given you the night off."

Oops, Max thought. "I guess the words *hollow center of the earth* should have tipped me off, huh?" he said. "I don't have much of a sense of humor tonight."

"Don't worry about it," Ray said. "And just for the record, as far as I know, you, me, Michael, and Isabel are the only aliens on earth."

"So what's this Hollow Earth Society deal?" Max asked. He wanted to check the time again, but he wouldn't let himself. If he kept thinking about Liz and Jerry, he really *would* need a lobotomy.

"Just one of the wackier human theories," Ray explained. "You want to hear about it—or you want to tell me what's got you in such a fever?"

"Nothing really to talk about," Max said. What was he supposed to say? That he was losing his mind because Liz—the girl he told he wanted to be just friends—was going out with someone else tonight?

"If you change your mind, you know where to find me." Ray glanced at his watch. "Blow the whistle—it's quitting time," he said. "You go ahead and take off. I'll close up."

"Thanks," Max said. He bolted out to his Jeep and swung into the driver's seat. Now what? he wondered. Go home and spend the night imagining Liz in Jerry's arms? He drummed his fingers on the steering wheel. I'll go to a movie, he decided. That will keep my mind off what Liz is doing with Jerry.

He pulled out onto the street and headed toward

the mall. When he made a left onto Cordova, he could see UFOnics' bright orange neon sign, with its spaceship crashing over and over. Max planned to just drive on by, he really did, but it was like the Jeep had a mind of its own.

Now what's the plan, you big idiot? Max asked himself as he maneuvered the Jeep into one of the last parking spots. He couldn't just go inside and stare at Liz.

Unless . . .

With a soft whispering sound his hair began to grow. Max stopped it when it got to his shoulders. Black, he decided. He tilted down the rearview mirror and watched as his blond hair turned a molted orange, then darkened to a muddy brown, and finally became a deep shiny black.

Not too shabby, Max thought. He couldn't do the changes as fast and smooth as Ray yet, but still, not too shabby. He turned his attention to his face, and his skin began to bubble. It didn't hurt or anything, but it looked repulsive. Max squeezed his eyes shut. When he opened them, his cheekbones were higher, his nose was smaller, and his skin was several shades darker.

What everyone at the Aliens Among Us conference downtown wouldn't give to see this, Max thought as he climbed out of the Jeep and headed inside. He promised himself he'd just take a quick look. He pushed his way through the crowd and found a spot at one of the little tables circling the dance floor. He hated the chairs in this place. They were designed to look like gigantic moon rocks and they always wobbled.

Craig Cachopo stalked up and asked Max what he wanted to drink. As much as he hated the chairs Max loved seeing some of the school elite dressed in the world's dweebiest, bad-sci-fi-meets-bad-disco-glitter uniforms. The expression on Craig's face made it absolutely clear that no comments on his shiny purple spandex space suit would be tolerated.

Max ordered a Lime Warp. He was actually starting to like them now that Ray had forced a few down his throat. When Craig stomped off in his orange half boots, Max saw what he came there to see but didn't really want to see—Liz and Jerry on the dance floor. At least it was a fast song, so he didn't have to see them actually touching.

She is so utterly beautiful, Max thought. Liz smiled at Jerry, and Max felt his heart constrict. He wished he could get a clearer look at her aura to see if she was enjoying herself as much as she seemed to be. But UFOnics' flashing colored lights made everyone's aura difficult to read.

Max drank three Lime Warps and ate an order of extreme pile-on-everything nachos, watching Liz every moment. With the face of some other guy he could stare at her as much as he wanted.

Liz and Jerry sat down at a nearby table, and Max kept his eyes locked on her. He realized he hadn't really looked at her in days. Lately when he talked to her, he kept his eyes focused slightly to the side of her face. That's how bad things had gotten between them, how awkward and uncomfortable. He had totally screwed up with that kiss at the mall. That heart-pounding kiss.

Liz glanced up—right at him. Her deep brown eyes locked on his as if she were staring straight into his soul.

Oh no, Max thought frantically. She'll kill me for following her here!

He looked away, pretending he hadn't seen her. She can't know it's me, he told himself. I'm completely disguised. She can't know.

When he allowed himself to look at her again, Liz was leaning close to Jerry, whispering something in his ear.

A slow song started up, and Max felt every muscle in his body tense. Were they going to dance? Liz stood up. Jerry reached out, like he was going to take her hand.

Max bolted. He shoved his way through the crowd and out into the cool night air. He'd seen enough. He didn't need to see Jerry put his arms around Liz, slide his fingers through her hair.

I could go back in there and stop it, Max thought suddenly. He could bump into Jerry, make a quick connection, and stimulate the acid production in Jerry's stomach or something. Not enough to really hurt him. Just enough to make sure he spent the rest of the night dancing with the toilet instead of Liz.

He immediately felt disgusted with himself. To even think about using his power to do harm was totally sick. He jammed his hands in his pockets and started toward the Jeep.

"Max," a voice called behind him.

He turned around and saw Liz. He had no trouble reading her aura this time. She was furious.

"I knew it was you," she said. "Did you forget that today at lunch you told us Ray taught you to change your appearance?"

Actually, he *had* forgotten. Should he deny it was him? Say he had no idea what she was talking about? There was no way she could be one hundred percent sure.

"You want a little tip?" Liz demanded. "Next time change your clothes, too. Did you think I wouldn't recognize your jacket? Oh, and change the eyes. I would know your eyes anywhere—" Her voice broke.

Then Liz took a step closer to him. So close, the edges of her aura started to blend with his. All he wanted to do was pull her up against him and feel her mouth under his.

"You know what, Max?" she asked, her voice harsh. "You could have been the one dancing with me in there. *You* made the choice to push me away. Now live with it." She whirled around and strode back into the club without looking back.

Why didn't Michael kiss me? Maria asked herself for about the one hundred and fifth time since she'd helped him baby-sit. She added another dollop of her special home-blended bath oil to the water—she liked to be surrounded in a cloud of scent—then settled back against her sponge pillow and closed her eyes. And kept thinking about Michael, of course.

He'd at least thought about kissing her. She knew that for sure. She'd seen the way his eyes flicked down to her lips. He had definitely been thinking about moving in.

Maria sighed, sending little ripples through the water. Okay, he *thought* about kissing her. That was good. It meant he didn't totally see her as a buddy or whatever.

So what was the problem? Maybe it was an alien-human thing. Maria would never forget how Nikolas used to look at her, when he looked at her at all. It was so clear he'd thought she was a lower life-form. Much lower.

No, that couldn't be it. Michael wouldn't come crawling through her window every couple of nights if he thought of her as half an evolutionary step above mold.

So what was the deal? What was holding him back? I should get Liz to help me figure him out, Maria thought. Except Liz was going through a romantic trauma right now. Maria knew it was pulverizing Liz's heart to go out with another guy because that meant starting to accept the fact that she and Max were never going to be together.

Maria didn't want to torture Liz by making her analyze why Maria couldn't get something started with Michael while Liz was trying to deal with everything *ending* with Max.

That's why Maria hadn't even told Liz about being psychic. If she told Liz about it, Liz would want to do a bunch of experiments to make sure that Maria's imagination hadn't taken off with her again. And she'd probably get all worried about the blacking-out thing. Maria wasn't worried. It was just a side effect. Perfectly harmless. No, she'd let Liz get some of her equilibrium back before she announced that Liz now had her very own psychic friend.

I could tell Michael about my psychic powers, she thought. He's not going through anything devastating the way Liz and Isabel are. He'd have time to help me explore my powers.

Yeah, and then I'd have the perfect excuse to talk to him, she realized. Maybe we could bond over what a kick it is to have superhuman powers. Maybe if he'd known I had powers, he would have kissed me.

What was Michael thinking right now? Was he thinking she was a loser for throwing herself at him?

You could take a little *peek* at him. You do still have his sweatshirt, Maria reminded herself. It was lying right next to the bathtub—and she had the ring on. She wore it all the time.

Maria reached down and touched the sweatshirt with one finger. This is wrong, she thought. But it wasn't a *big* wrong. It was a little wrong. She only wanted to take a fast look, just to see if she could get any clue about what was going on in Michael's so-called brain.

I'm doing it, she decided. Where is Michael—

Before she completed the thought, the bathtub dissolved into colored dots. When they clumped, they formed a warm white mist. Maria could hear the sound of running water.

She peered through the mist and made out the outlines of a glass door. And on the other side of that door Michael was taking a shower.

Maria started to giggle. Michael would really think

100

she was throwing herself at him if he could see her right now. Thank God, he couldn't.

The tile floor wiggled under her feet, and a few moments later she was back in the bathtub. She turned on the hot water with her toes and warmed up her bath. She let herself slide completely underwater, her hair floating around her face.

Why was the water so cold?

Maria tried to sit up, but she couldn't move. She lay on the bottom of the tub, her body as heavy as lead. Water covered her nose, her mouth.

She felt a tightness in her lungs. She needed to take a breath. There was plenty of air inches away. But she couldn't move inches. She couldn't move at all.

I'm going to drown, Maria thought wildly. I'm going to drown in my own bathtub!

Kevin and her mother wouldn't hear a single splash. Because she couldn't move.

Her lungs began to burn. Her lungs were on fire.

How long did she have? Another minute? Two?

Maria's vision darkened, turning the water above her black.

This is it. This is where I die.

Liz saw Jerry smile as she walked toward him. Good. The absolute rage boiling inside her must not show. It wouldn't be fair to make Jerry deal with *that*.

Max. He was the guy who deserved to have her fury come pouring down on his head like lava. He deserved to have to stand in that parking lot for hours listening to Liz tell him what a total and complete jerk he was.

He had gotten off way too easily. That's because if Liz had tried to say one more word to him, she would have burst into tears. And that's not something she'd wanted to do in front of him. No, the crying would have to wait until she got home and got into the shower. She didn't cry much, but when she did, the shower was her place. She would adjust the spray so it came down in those stinging needles and let the hot water wash away her tears— and drown out any sounds. She never let her parents hear her when she cried. Never.

"So *was* he the kid from your kindergarten class?" Jerry asked when she reached him.

Liz shook her head. "Nope. It was a total stranger. I made a fool of myself."

"Yeah, poor guy," Jerry said. "Having some gorgeous girl chase him out to the parking lot." He took a long drink of his planet punch and stared at the dance floor. It was obvious he was embarrassed by what he'd just said.

He's so sweet, Liz thought. He shouldn't be here with her. He should be here with a girl who didn't have ninety-nine percent of her brain focused on some other guy.

Suddenly the music screeched to a stop. The club went black. The crowd gave a long *aaah* of anticipation, then a loud voice came over the PA. "Okay, everyone. It's that time—time for the alien bop!"

The alien bop. Roswell's answer to the bunny hop. As if the bunny hop needed any kind of answer. Liz could *not* figure out how it had become this hugely popular thing.

"I have something to tell you. I should have told you before," Jerry said as people began to make long, snaking lines through the club. He leaned closer. "I don't bop."

Liz laughed. A real laugh. "Me neither," she admitted.

It was a moment. One of those times when two people were totally in sync. Liz had them all the time with Max. At least she used to.

"Let's sit down fast," Liz said. She spotted a free table and led the way over to it. She cautiously perched on one of the wobbly moon rock chairs just as the bopping got started.

"Okay, it's time for the judging," Jerry said. "I get to be the East German judge. You can be the Swedish

103

judge." He scanned the long line of alien boppers weaving around the tables.

"See that girl over there?" He tilted his head toward a tall girl dressed in a white shirt and pressed khakis. "I give her a ten for technique. See how she's always on the right foot and how she never breaks her grip on the person in front of her? But she only gets a two for originality. She's not letting enough of *her* shine through. She's not *owning* the bop."

Liz laughed again. It felt good. Maybe she wouldn't need a crying session in the shower after all. Maria was right, Liz thought. I'm glad she talked me into doing this.

"The guy over there has the opposite problem," Liz said. She pointed, trying not to be too obvious. "He's so original, I don't think he's even doing the same dance as everybody else."

"So what's his score?" Jerry asked.

"Hmmm. I'd say originality—an eleven. Technique— a minus three. And for the tattoo—four bonus points because I love a guy who's not afraid to walk around with a koala bear on his arm."

Jerry shook his head. "I don't know who let you on this panel. You can't just throw points around like that. Bop judging is a serious responsibility. You're deciding who gets the multimillion-dollar contract to do Cosmic Crunch commercials and who goes home with only a bucketful of shame."

Liz laughed so hard, she snorted. She didn't think Jerry heard because the room had erupted in the post-bop hooting and cheering. When the crowd finally calmed down, a slow song started up.

"You want to?" Jerry asked.

"Sure," she answered. The touching thing . . . it didn't feel like so much of a thing anymore. It was just a dance. She didn't know why she'd been so weirded out by the idea. What was the big deal?

"You positive you don't want to get some air, or go to the bathroom, or get a soda?" he teased.

Uh-oh. Jerry had caught on to her no-slow-dance strategy. "I'm sorry—," she began.

"It's okay," he interrupted. "I'm sort of shy, too."

Sort of. Liz remembered how she had pegged Jerry as a *sort-of* guy. But it wasn't true. Now that she'd gotten to know him a little, she realized there was nothing *sort of* about him.

Jerry held out his hand, and Liz took it. His fingers felt a little sweaty—he was nervous, she realized. He found a corner of the dance floor that wasn't totally crammed with people, then he slid his arms around her back and held her lightly. He didn't try to pull her up against him, and he didn't let his hands wander too low, the way some guys did.

Liz rested her head on Jerry's shoulder. That way there wouldn't be any awkward moment when he moved in for a kiss and she pulled away. She hoped Jerry didn't notice that she was holding herself a little stiffly. She was having a hard time getting comfortable. Jerry's shoulder was the wrong height for her or something. The muscles in her neck felt all tense.

Liz closed her eyes and took a deep breath. Jerry was wearing some kind of musky aftershave. It made her nose itch. And his shirt was sort of rough under her cheek. Ever heard of fabric softener? she thought, and immediately felt bad.

She could feel Jerry's heart pounding against her cheek. It was beating so fast. And hers wasn't. Because she was totally calm.

It didn't take a rocket scientist to figure out why— Jerry wasn't Max.

When the song ended, Liz gently pulled away. "Would you mind if we left?" she asked. "I'm not feeling that well. I need to go home."

Yeah. She needed to go home so she could take a long, hot shower.

I'm going to die, Maria thought.

She felt the water enter her nose, trickle down her throat. I'm going to die.

Then she was free. Her body was under her control again. She scrambled to her feet, sliding on the wet porcelain.

She hauled in a deep breath of air and coughed, spitting water. When her legs felt steady enough, she carefully climbed out of the tub. She wrapped her bath sheet around her and sank down on the floor. She needed to rest for a minute before she could even walk across the hall to her room.

That was lethally stupid, she thought. She knew she lost time every time she used her psychic powers. And she decided to go spy on Michael while lying in the *bathtub*. Stupid, stupid, stupid.

Maria grabbed another towel off the rack above her and scrubbed her face with it. She wanted every drop of water off her. She ripped open the cabinet under the sink and yanked out her blow-dryer. She leaned across the room and plugged it in. She pulled off the diffuser and turned the dryer to high. She didn't care that it would turn her hair into a matted mess. She needed to be dry right now. Completely dry

She held the dryer so close to her scalp, she felt it starting to burn. She had to calm down. She clicked off the dryer and pushed herself to her feet. She sprayed a little conditioner into her hair, the kind you could leave in, then gently started pulling a comb through her wild curls.

See, you're okay, she told herself. Probably because the water hitting her face made her come out of her blackout faster than usual. You're okay. It's not a problem. You just have to be more careful next time.

Yeah, she was okay. But she could have died.

Alex made a left onto her street. Isabel wished he would keep driving. She didn't care where. She loved sitting next to him in his little VW Rabbit. It felt so cozy and secure.

"Do you want to come in?" she asked when he pulled up in front of her house.

"I should get going," Alex said. "My dad believes in getting an early start on things. He'll probably roust me out of bed at six. By noon he'll be doing the old white glove test on the garage, then after lunch I'm scheduled to start in on the basement."

Isabel felt a knot tighten in her stomach. Both her

parents' cars were in the driveway, and Max's Jeep was parked on the street. So it's not like she'd be alone when she went inside or anything. But she just felt better when she was around Alex, like nothing bad could happen to her as long as she was with him.

"I could come by and help you tomorrow," Isabel volunteered, partly because she really did want to spend the day with him and partly just to keep him talking so she could stay with him a little longer.

"I think my dad would consider you more of a distraction than a help," Alex said.

Isabel popped open the glove compartment. "I'm always curious to see what guys keep in their cars," she said. Which was a total lie. But she studied the license and registration, gum wrappers, penlight, map, and loose change, anyway. She just wasn't ready to get out of the car.

And Alex shouldn't be ready to *let* her get out. Isabel crossed her legs, hoping the move might remind Alex that yes, there was a real live girl in his car. She wasn't used to having to give hints. So what was going on? Why was Alex over there with his hands locked on the steering wheel when he could have his hands on her? She knew he was gaga over her. There had been days when she'd practically had to step around pools of his drool when she walked past him.

I must have flipped Alex out when I started crying on him the other day, she thought. She'd definitely flipped *herself* out.

It had felt like Alex accidentally pressed some "tears" button when he touched her. She hadn't been feeling sad or anything, at least she didn't remember feeling sad, but suddenly *whoosh,* the floodgates opened.

"Um, I really have to take off," Alex said. "I'll talk to you tomorrow."

"Oh. Okay. Bye." She wasn't going to *beg* him to let her stay in the car. Isabel climbed out and gently shut the door behind her. She started up the walkway, then hesitated. Maybe she should do something to show Alex that she wasn't going to lose it if they kissed again.

Isabel turned around and rushed back to the car. She tapped on Alex's window, and he rolled it down. "I, uh, forgot to say good night."

"Oh, yeah, good—" Before Alex could finish, Isabel took his face in her hands and kissed him. She caught him with his mouth half open, so she deepened their kiss instantly.

He kissed her back for about half a second, then he pulled away. He cleared his throat. "I don't think . . . I don't think this is a great idea," he said.

"You're still parked." Isabel tried to keep her tone light and teasing even though the lump in her stomach had just doubled. "There wasn't much chance I was going to make you have an accident."

"That's not what I meant," he answered.

"Well, what *did* you mean?" Isabel asked.

"I just can't deal with kissing you—not when I know you're thinking about . . . someone else," Alex answered slowly. "I completely understand, though. And I want to stay friends," he added. "We can still hang out and stuff."

"And stuff. Oh, good. I'd hate to miss the stuff," Isabel mumbled. She felt like someone had just grabbed a baseball bat and smacked her on the head with it. She was reeling, hardly able to keep on her feet.

Alex had rejected her. *Alex*—the guy who was at least three rungs below her on the school social scale. How pathetic. How humiliating. How . . . unacceptable.

Isabel forced a laugh. "Well, that's a relief," she said. "So I guess I'm off the hook?"

Alex's eyes clouded over with confusion. "What do you mean?"

"Well, duh," she said. "I was only being nice to you because you helped save my life. I mean, you're a charity case. You know that, right?"

Alex studied her for a moment, his green eyes serious. Then he shook his head. "You're going to have to do better than that," he said. "I'll call you tomorrow night."

Isabel stared after his car as he drove off. Alex had looked *disappointed* in her. She turned and ran for the house. Trying to make it inside before the tears came.

Michael led Maria into his room. "We have to leave the door open," he told her. "That's rule number forty-seven on the Pascals' list."

"So I guess we'll just have to eat our pudding, not wrestle around naked in it," Maria teased.

Michael choked on the big spoonful of pudding he'd just shoveled into his mouth. Whoa. That image almost knocked his thoughts up into the X-rated zone. And he'd been doing pretty well up until now. He'd been relieved when Maria had shown up wearing those baggy overalls for the Pascals' we-want-to-meet-one-of-Michael's-friends dinner. The outfit helped keep his mind where it should be. Well, except for the fact that he kept getting glimpses of the tiny T-shirt she was wearing underneath the overalls. The overalls put Maria in the cute category. But the T-shirt, the T-shirt kept trying to push her over into sexy.

Maria plopped down on Dylan's bed and glanced around the room. Michael leaned against his dresser. "I see you haven't taken my advice and started watching Martha Stewart," she commented. "You need *one* personal thing in here at least. If you don't get one, I'm going to give you one—maybe a nice ceramic raccoon, in honor of the Pascals."

"I have CDs and books," Michael protested. "What do you want from me?" Maria had lived in the same house since she was born. She didn't understand that when you moved from place to place, you couldn't haul a bunch of junk with you.

"Doesn't count," she insisted. "I'm going shopping tomorrow. I'm going to find the very best raccoon for you. Maybe one with a little top hat."

"Wait." Michael opened his top dresser drawer. "Here's one thing I do have." He pulled out a piece of what looked like metal about the size of a book of matches and handed it to her. "It's from the ship. At least I think it is—I've never even *heard* of anything like it. Try crinkling it up."

Maria stared at him, then at the material in her palm. She tightened her hand around it, squeezing the metal into a little ball. The moment she opened her fingers, the metal straightened itself out into exactly the same shape it had been before. It didn't even have one tiny dent. "Wow," she whispered.

"That's why I think the ship is still out there somewhere," Michael told her. "If it's made of that stuff, it has to be pretty much indestructible. I've tried everything on that piece—hammer, saw, even a blowtorch. Nothing hurts it."

"Can I try something?" Maria asked.

Michael laughed. "Go ahead, muscle girl. Maybe I just wasn't strong enough."

Maria shook her head, her blond curls bouncing

around her face. "Not that. I . . ." She hesitated for a moment. "This is going to sound flaky—"

"Flaky, you? No way," Michael joked.

Maria didn't laugh. "I'm serious," she said. "I think there might be a way I can help you find the ship."

Michael was sure Maria was serious. The same way she was serious about her aromatherapy, and her plant extracts, and everything else. But there was no way she could—

"You don't believe me, do you?" Maria asked, interrupting his thoughts. "Look, it is pretty strange, but a few days ago I realized I have this *talent*. I can touch an object and get images from it. Like I held Liz's lipstick—and then I *saw* her at the mall. I saw what she was doing because I was holding her lipstick. I've never tried holding a piece of something and, you know, *looking* for the whole thing. But it might work."

Huh? Michael thought. What was she talking about?

"Um . . ." What was he supposed to say? He didn't want to hurt Maria's feelings. Obviously she believed every ridiculous word coming out of her raspberry-colored mouth.

"I'm going to try it. I just want to try it, okay?" she said in a rush.

"Okay," Michael answered. "Do you need some incense? I think Mrs. Pascal has some basil leaves or something we could burn," he said. Maybe if he joked around a little now, it wouldn't be so bad for Maria when *whatever* she was going to try didn't work.

"I don't need anything except this." She held up the piece of metal and stared at it. "Oh!" She turned back to him. "I get sort of . . . paralyzed for a few minutes right after I do the seeing—I can't move or talk. So don't call 911 or anything. Try splashing some water on my face. I think that helps me get out faster."

"Carbonated or noncarbonated?" Michael asked.

Maria didn't answer. She closed her eyes and whispered, "Where is the ship?"

Nothing happened. At least nothing that Michael could see. Maria just sat there, still and quiet. Then her eyes started to move under her closed lids.

Michael folded his arms across his chest. What was going on? Was she actually *seeing* something? That wasn't possible, was it?

Maria's eyes snapped open. "I saw it! I saw the ship!" she exclaimed. "It was—"

She stopped midsentence, her mouth dropping open. Her blue eyes lost their sparkle. Her face became as expressionless as a mask.

Michael felt his stomach tighten as he watched her. She's like a zombie, he thought. She's sitting here breathing and everything, but all the Maria-ness has been sucked out of her.

Water. He needed water. He raced down the hall to the bathroom, grabbed one of the little paper cups from the dispenser, filled it, and ran back. He threw the cupful of water in Maria's face.

Nothing happened. What was he supposed to do now? Maybe he didn't use enough water. He started toward the door, then heard Maria gasp. He turned around in time to see her give a little twitch. Then she looked over at him and smiled a total Maria smile, her eyes bright and alive. Michael felt relief spread through him.

"Are you all right?" he demanded. He sank down on the bed next to her.

"I'm fine. And I saw the ship!" Maria cried, grabbing his arm.

She sounded okay. And she did seem back to normal. But this whole psychic powers thing was still hard to swallow. "Tell me what you, um, saw," Michael said.

"A huge cement warehouse, as big as the mall, maybe bigger," Maria began. "A guard was posted in front of it. A pretty heavy-duty guard—with a machine gun strapped across his chest."

Michael listened carefully. What Maria was describing sounded like a scene from some dumb sci-fi movie about government conspiracies. She *did* have a pretty active imagination. Maybe she thought she was seeing the ship when really she was remembering some fictional thing she'd seen once.

"What kind of uniform was the guard wearing?" he asked. Maybe he could figure out which movie she was remembering.

Maria made a face. "Totally plain gray," she said. "And he looked really bored. He was cute, though."

Hmmm. If the guard had been some actor, Maria probably would have realized it. Maybe she *had* seen something. Maybe she did have psychic power. Stranger things had happened.

And if she had powers, maybe she really was seeing their parents' ship! Michael desperately wanted to believe that she was seeing their ship.

"Were there any windows?" he asked. "Could you see anything outside that would give us a clue about the warehouse's location?"

Maria shook her head. "No windows."

It could be anywhere, Michael realized. The warehouse could be underground in the desert. Or it could be in DC. It could be in South Africa or China or . . . anywhere. It really could be anywhere.

Maria moved her hand gently up to his shoulder. "Guess that wasn't much help, huh?"

"Well, if you really saw it, then at least I know for sure the ship exists, that it wasn't destroyed," Michael said. He tried to hide his doubt and disappointment. He didn't want Maria to feel bad.

"But you knew that already," she said softly. "Like you said, this is indestructible."

Maria handed the little piece of metal back to him. Michael shoved it deep into his pocket. That scrap of debris from the crash might be the closest he'd ever get to his parents' ship.

"I don't know why I even care anymore," he told Maria. "Ray told us they were all dead. He told us to think of earth as our home. I just wish . . . I just want to see it for myself, you know? Touch something my parents touched."

Maria took his hand. Her warm, smooth fingers touching his skin snapped him out of his thoughts about the ship. He gazed into her blue eyes.

116

"If I had something of the guard's, I might be able to find out more," Maria told him.

"How would that help you see anything different than what you just described?" Michael asked. "The guard is in the same windowless warehouse."

"Yeah, but not always," Maria answered. "Sometimes the guard's on his *way* to the warehouse. If I *saw* him then, I might be able to get some landmarks," she explained.

But finding the guard would be as hard as finding the ship, Michael thought. The guard could be in the desert or DC or South America or China, too.

"I guess if you knew how to find the guard, you wouldn't really need my help, though, huh?" Maria said, echoing his thought.

She sounded really bummed. Michael studied her face. She looked tired and sad. Maria was like that. When you were her friend, it was like what happened to you happened to her. She cared that much.

"I should get home," Maria said. "Remember to ask Dylan how the dance went. And get details. Guys never bother to get the details."

She grabbed her purse. Well, actually it was a beat-up lunch box—one of the old metal ones. It had a picture of Miss America on the front. Definitely G rated.

"Details. Right," Michael answered as he followed her out of the room and down the hall to the front door.

"Nice to meet you, Maria," Mr. Pascal called from the living room.

"You too," Maria called back.

"I'll walk you out," Michael told her. He led the way to her car. They both hesitated when they reached it. "Are you sure you're okay?" Michael asked. "I hated the way you looked when you were paralyzed."

"I'm fine. I just wish I could have helped," she answered. She opened her lunch box purse and pulled out her keys. Then she stood there, jingling them in her fingers.

The image of Maria with her arms around him as they danced in the living room shoved its way into his mind. Had she really wanted him to kiss her last night? Did she want him to kiss her *now?* Was that why she was just standing there, not making a move to get into the car?

Maybe he should do it. A fast good-night kind of kiss. Nothing major. A test to see if the little-sister feeling came rushing at him. If he was really careful about duration of lip-to-lip contact, he might not even completely cross over into the something-more-than-friends zone. There was such a thing as a friendly kiss, wasn't there?

He took a quick glance around the street to see if anyone was watching—and spotted Sheriff Valenti's cruiser gliding toward them. He heard Maria give a little squeak, so he knew she'd seen it, too.

Valenti continued past without slowing down. "That guy is everywhere," Maria said.

"Yeah," Michael agreed. "He doesn't want a dog peeing on a fire hydrant that he doesn't know about. I bet *he* knows where my parents' ship is."

He and Maria locked eyes, and he knew they'd

had exactly the same thought at exactly the same time. If they could get something of Valenti's, Maria could use it to do her *seeing* thing on him.

"Michael—," she began.

He nodded. "I guess I'll need to pay a visit to the sheriff sometime soon."

"You mean *we* will," Maria corrected him.

"And after we snag a pair of his boxers or whatever, you can just *check in* on Valenti a couple of times a day until you find out what we need to know," Michael continued.

"I'm not touching Valenti's boxers—even for you," Maria joked. Then her expression grew serious. "But it might take a while to get any good info." She sounded worried.

"Hey, it will be a lot quicker than crawling over every inch of the desert the way I've been doing," Michael answered. His odds of finding the ship had gotten much, much better in the last few minutes, thanks to Maria.

She unlocked her car door and climbed in. She rolled down the window. "Okay, so we have a plan," she said. "I'm spending the day with Kevin and my dad tomorrow—a visitation rights thing—but after that we can get started."

He felt like doing one of Maria's wild happy dances. He was going to find his parents' ship. He knew it. He was going home!

Except . . . except it wouldn't be much of a home with no family there waiting for him. He'd be surrounded by a bunch of strangers.

Maria gave a little beep on the horn as she pulled away from the curb. Michael waved to her.

Maybe Max and Isabel would go with me, he thought. Yeah, that would be cool, taking in the sights with Izzy and Max. He smiled at the picture.

Then his smile faded. Max would never leave earth, not while Liz was here. And Isabel had decided to live the rest of her life as just a "normal human girl," whatever that meant. And besides, if he did get the ship to work, if he did return to their home planet, he'd be leaving Maria, and Liz, and Alex behind. The three humans had become almost as close to him as Max and Isabel. Losing them . . . Michael didn't even want to think about the hole that would rip inside him.

He stared down the deserted street. Maria's car had disappeared. He pulled down the sleeves of his sweatshirt. It was colder out than he thought.

Maybe he should have kissed Maria. That would have kept him warm.

"A nematode, for example, can dry up and turn crispy. Crispy—that's a scientific term," Ms. Hardy told the class. "But when it's put into water, it comes back to life."

Just call me Mr. Nematode, Max thought. Because when Liz wasn't around, he could feel himself drying up inside until he was half dead. And then when he saw her . . . total reanimation.

"Here's how it works. When the nematode dries out, its cells make a special compound," Ms. Hardy said.

Max tried to pay attention to the teacher's explanation, but his eyes kept drifting back to Liz. She had her head lowered as she took notes, her long hair forming a curtain that hid most of her face from his view.

But he didn't need to see her face to know how she was feeling. Her aura said it all. The deep red bolts of fury that he'd seen in it outside UFOnics had faded. But what had replaced them was even worse— the oily gray-green of deep sadness now covered her entire aura. Liz was miserable.

And it was all his fault. From the day he first told

her his secret, he'd been screwing up her life. He'd put her in danger from Valenti, that was bad enough. But then he'd messed with her head—kissing her, then telling her they had to be just friends, then kissing her *again*, then telling her they had to be just friends *again*. Could he have hurt her any more if he'd spent months coming up with some master plan? He didn't think so.

The least he could have done was leave her alone after all that—even if it did make him feel like he was drying up inside. But no, he had to pull that psycho stalker boy stunt. The next time Liz was out with a guy, she'd probably spend the whole time scanning the crowd, trying to figure out which one was Max.

He had to admit part of him—the big, ugly, selfish part—liked the idea of Liz ignoring other guys, even for such a twisted reason. But Max wasn't going to let that part rule him. He was going to do the right thing. If it made him crumble into a pile of gritty dust, well, too bad for him. He deserved it.

Max forced himself to tune into Ms. Hardy again. "Answer the questions on page forty-two for Wednesday," she said.

The bell rang. Liz shoved her notebook in her backpack and bolted. She obviously did not want one more second of Max contact than was absolutely necessary. She'd even skipped lunch in the quad today.

Max grabbed his stuff and took off after her. "Liz, wait," he called, running out into the hall. He realized a second too late that she'd been talking to Jerry.

Great. He had to end up doing one more thing to make himself look like a total jerk, right?

Liz spun around and strode back over to him, her dark eyes glittering with anger. "You better be calling me to say you're moving to another state," she snapped. "Otherwise I'm out of here."

"Just listen to me for one second," he begged. She didn't say no, so he started talking as fast as he could. "I'm sorry about what happened on Friday night."

"I really, really don't want to listen to another apology from you," Liz interrupted. "If you're sorry, prove it—leave me alone."

"I will. I promise. That's what I wanted to tell you," Max answered. He hesitated, not wanting to say this next part. But he was the one who kept telling Liz they had to be just friends. So right now he was going to actually do that—be her friend, and help un-screw up her life.

"And . . . and I also wanted to say that I've hung out with Jerry a little and he's a good guy," Max told her. "I think you two would be a good couple."

"Thanks for giving us your blessing," she said sarcastically. "I wouldn't want to be with a guy *you* didn't approve of."

Max could hardly listen to what she was saying. His eyes were locked on the black splotches of pain exploding in her aura.

He'd just hurt her again. Hurt her worse than he ever had before.

Isabel tried to remember what Alex's last class was. If she hurried, maybe she could catch him coming out. Or maybe it would be better to go straight to the parking lot and find his Rabbit.

We can use that free game coupon I won last time we went miniature golfing, she thought. I guess I should apologize for calling him a charity case first. Then after golf we can go to the Crashdown and—

Stop it, she ordered herself. Just stop it. She couldn't keep using Alex. That's what she'd been doing—using him, using him to keep away the memories, to help her feel safe, to make her feel like an ordinary human girl who barely knew what Sheriff Valenti looked like.

Alex deserved better. And so did she. What, was she some pathetic loser who needed a guy to take care of her? Isabel didn't think so. And she was going to prove it—right now. She was going to the mall. She was going to the place where Nikolas died. It was time to get over this thing.

She hurried down the halls and out the school's big double doors. She didn't notice Liz and Maria hanging out in the quad until Maria grabbed her arm.

"Hey, Isabel," Maria said. "How're you doing?"

"Great," she answered. But one look at Maria's face told her that Maria wasn't going to buy it. Isabel sighed. "Actually, not so good," she admitted. "I'm still thinking about Nikolas all the time. I . . . I was going to go to the mall. I wanted to look at the last places we went together. I don't know, I thought maybe it would help me get some closure or something."

"We'll go with you," Liz immediately volunteered.

"Yeah, you can't go alone," Maria said. "Come on.

I see the bus." She grabbed Isabel by the arm and they ran to the bus stop, Liz right behind them.

Maria led the way onto the bus, and they found seats together in the last row. Isabel stared at her friends in surprise. She hadn't expected Liz and Maria to sympathize with her—they had both hated Nikolas.

"Thanks . . . thanks for going with me," she said. "I know the mall doesn't exactly have great memories for you two, either."

The night Nikolas had died, Isabel had been way too out of it to realize Liz and Maria were at the mall. The only one she even remembered being around after Nikolas got shot was Max. But they had both been there, searching for her, trying to get to her before Valenti did.

Liz and Maria were both quiet for a moment. "Yeah," Liz finally said. "That was not a good night."

"I never said I was sorry," Isabel said. "Not for what you went through that night . . . or before." Nikolas had treated Liz and Maria with total contempt. He'd used his power to knock Liz out, just to prove a point. And Isabel had walked around insisting it was okay because Nikolas didn't really hurt Liz.

"That's right. You didn't," Maria answered.

"Can I say it now? Is it too late?" Isabel asked.

"I think you can just get in under the apology expiration date," Liz said. Maria nodded.

Isabel felt her eyes fill with tears. They were willing to forgive her. "I'm sorry," she said. "I don't know how to say it any better. I shouldn't have let Nikolas treat you the way he did. And I should have listened when you all told me he was putting me in danger."

"Well, you were in love with him," Liz said.

"Yeah. It's not like you're the first girl who ever did something stupid because she was in love," Maria added.

Isabel managed a little smile. "You're both being so nice to me," she said, her voice breaking.

"What did you expect?" Liz demanded. "Did you think we'd dump you as a friend because you did one dumb—one very dumb—thing?"

"Actually, it did cross my mind," Isabel admitted.

"You're nuts," Maria said. "Maybe that would happen with casual friends, but we're a lot more than that. Think about that connection Max made between us. That made us more than friends. It's like we're almost sisters—you know, fristers."

"Yeah," Liz agreed. "The three of us are fristers."

Fristers. Isabel liked the sound of that. She liked it a lot.

"This is our stop," Liz said.

Isabel stared out the window as the bus pulled up at the mall. Her stomach tightened.

"I want to go to Macy's first," she told Liz and Maria as they climbed off the bus.

"Are you sure?" Maria asked.

Isabel nodded. If she was going to do this, she was going to do it all the way. She was going to go right to the spot where Valenti shot Nikolas.

She took the lead as they entered the store. She strode directly to the formal wear department, not even glancing at the racks of sportswear or the other shoppers.

"I think I want to go the rest of the way by myself," she said.

"Okay, Maria and I will go over to the phones by the elevators," Liz said. "I should call my mom and tell her where I am, anyway. Take as long as you want."

"Yeah. Take as long as you want. But if you're not over to the phones in fifteen minutes, we're coming to get you," Maria added.

"Thanks," Isabel answered. She walked back to the dressing rooms without hesitation. She slipped behind the red curtain shielding the entrance and stood exactly where she had when she watched Valenti murder Nikolas. She peered out at the spot where he had fallen.

The patch of carpet looked just slightly darker than the rest. They'd obviously put in a new piece. The scent of gunpowder grew so strong, she could almost taste it in her mouth. You're imagining it, she reminded herself. You're only imagining it.

Isabel brought her hands to her chest. She started to pick at the polish on her thumbnail. Then she laced her hands tightly together. She wasn't going to start that again. She was going to stand here, just stand here, and look at the spot where Nikolas died.

She let the movie play in her head without trying to block it out, watching Nikolas fall to the ground again, and again, and again. Smelling the gunpowder.

"Can I help you?" a chilly voice asked.

Isabel turned around and saw a saleswoman staring at her. She must have come from one of the dressing rooms.

"I'm just . . . I'm just looking for a friend," Isabel answered. She turned back around and peered out at the dark patch of carpet again. No movie began in her head. The only odor she smelled was the chalky, musty scent of the curtain. "I guess he isn't here," she added softly.

I did it, she thought. I came here, I looked, and I survived. She pushed her way through the curtain and rushed over to the phones.

"I just want to go to a few more places," she told Liz and Maria. "First the jewelry store."

It was one of the last places she'd been with Nikolas. That's why she wanted to go there. She wanted to remember something besides the way he died, kind of relive their last hours together.

"Lead the way," Maria said.

Isabel hurried out the exit that led into the mall. She breathed in the smell of chocolate cookies from the stand across the way. There wasn't the slightest taint of gunpowder in the delicious scent. She pulled in a long, deep sniff.

She, Liz, and Maria strolled down the main walkway to the jewelry store, then went inside and wandered from counter to counter. Liz and Maria didn't try to get her to talk or anything. They just kept her company. It's like they knew she needed time to remember.

The last time she'd been here, she and Nikolas had had the store to themselves. They'd had the whole mall to themselves. She hadn't known how close Valenti was to finding them. She hadn't known Nikolas only had a few hours left to live.

"I'm ready to move on," Isabel told Maria and Liz.

"Do what you need to do," Liz answered. "We'll be right behind you."

Isabel led the way out of the store and up the escalator to the second floor. She hurried down to the drugstore and went to the old photo booth they had in the back.

She stood there, staring at it. Liz and Maria didn't ask any questions. They just stood with her.

This was the last place she and Nikolas had kissed. And it had been a good kiss, too. Wild and intense—just like Nikolas. Isabel wished she could stop her memories of that night right here.

But it was right after Nikolas kissed her that last time that their awesome night started to turn bad. "Nikolas and I were back here and we heard a security guard," she blurted. She'd wanted to tell somebody this since it happened. "Nikolas told me that I had to knock the guard out. He said if I didn't, he'd let us get caught."

Isabel wrapped her arms around her waist. She kept her eyes locked on the photo booth. She wanted to tell Liz and Maria what happened, but she couldn't look at their faces.

"I didn't want to do it," she continued. "But I was scared. Nikolas would have let the guard find us. I know it. So I jumped out and I did it. I hurt him. I could feel myself hurting him."

"Michael and Alex and I found him," Maria said. "Michael checked him. He was still out, but he was okay."

"That's not even the worst part," Isabel told them. She didn't know if Liz and Maria would still want to call themselves her fristers after they heard the rest.

"The worst part is I told Nikolas knocking out the guard was a rush," Isabel admitted. "I wanted him to think I was *fun*. Nikolas only wanted to hang out with me when I was *fun*. Otherwise, forget it."

"Oh, Isabel," Maria whispered. "That's awful. Awful for you, I mean. You loved him, and he treated you . . ." Maria let her words trail off.

He treated me totally unlike the way Alex does, Isabel thought. She tried to remember the last time *he* had any fun in her presence. It had to be that night they went miniature golfing because after she met Nikolas, Alex and the others didn't have any fun of any kind. But none of them walked away. And Alex . . . he'd been her walking, talking security blanket.

There's no way Nikolas would have sat outside her door, telling her goofy stories until his throat went dry just to make her feel better. And if she cried in front of Nikolas even once, he probably would have told her to call him when she was out of diapers.

"I'm going to go in there for a minute," Isabel said. She slipped into the photo booth and sat down on the little stool. She closed the curtain behind her and sighed.

She'd been thinking about Nikolas so much lately.

But only about the horrible way he died. He didn't deserve that—no one could possibly deserve that.

But would she even still be with Nikolas if he were alive? Would she still be doing back flips trying to show him how fun she was, trying to prove she wasn't a loser? And getting the hottest kisses ever? She couldn't forget that part.

Not that Alex left her cold or anything. Not hardly. She remembered the homecoming dance, when he'd run his fingers over the bare skin right above her dress's low back. Whoa.

Isabel dug some change out of her bag. She figured Alex deserved a little present for being such a good guy. And what could be a better present than pictures of her?

Isabel slid the change into the slot and pushed the start button. I'm going to be thinking of Alex in every one of these pictures, she promised herself. No one but Alex.

Maria heard a knock at her window. She knew it could only be Michael—everyone else used the front door. She jumped up from her desk and opened the window for him.

"I can't come in. I have to go to work. But I wanted to give you this," Michael told her. He handed her a pen.

Maria raised her eyebrows. "Thanks, I guess," she said. "It's never exactly been a dream of mine to have a pen where a centerfold loses her bathing suit." She tilted the pen back and forth, watching the little bikini slide off and on.

Michael laughed. "Really? It's always been a dream of mine," he said. Then his face turned serious. "It's Valenti's," he told her. "I snagged it out of his office."

Maria could practically feel ice cubes forming in her blood. "You promised that you wouldn't go alone. Michael, what if he caught you? What if—"

"Nothing happened," he said.

"But it could have," she shot back. She didn't care if Michael didn't want to hear this. He was going to. "If you didn't think I could handle it, which I totally could have, you should have brought Max or Alex."

"It seemed easier to do it myself," he answered. "You can yell at me more later if you really have to."

Maria shook her head. She really shouldn't be surprised that he decided to do a solo mission. That was a classic Michael move.

"Let me try it one time before you go. It will only take a second," she said.

"Okay, but wait. I want to get some water," Michael said. He hauled himself through the window.

"I have one of those sports bottles right there." She pointed to her dresser. Then she tightened her grip on the pen.

"Where's Valenti?" she asked.

The colored dots tornadoed around her. Then they clumped, and she found herself standing in a seriously messy kitchen with Valenti and his son, Kyle. She knew they couldn't see her, but it still freaked her out to be so close to Valenti.

"What's the problem, Kyle?" Valenti asked. "Are the dishes too heavy for you to move to the dishwasher? Or is it just that you get confused with all the shiny buttons you have to choose from?"

The dots swirled again, and Maria was back in her own room. She only had a moment before the paralysis took over her body. Since that night in the bathtub, she had stopped blacking out after using her power. Now she was aware of everything that happened, but she just couldn't move. She'd liked the blackouts better.

Maria watched Michael snatch the sports bottle off her dresser. She watched him aim it at her face. She couldn't even blink as the water hit her face. At least the water broke her out of the spell.

She wiped off the water with her sleeve. "I didn't see anything good," she told Michael. "Just Valenti chewing out Kyle." She never got to look at anyone for long, but this time she'd seen more than she wanted to in those few seconds. Kyle was a complete jerk, but Maria couldn't help feeling sort of sorry for him. Valenti's comment to his son had been so nasty.

"I wouldn't have minded seeing that," Michael said. He climbed back out the window. "I've got to go. We're having a sale on alien boxing puppets tomorrow. I have to change all the prices."

"I'll keep trying," Maria promised him.

"No! I mean, I don't want you to do it by yourself," Michael said, frowning. "Wait until I can be with you. The way you get paralyzed freaks me out."

Maria smiled. Whether he thought of her as a little sister or not, Michael definitely cared about her. "I'm fine," she told him. "Stop stressing or I'll have to make you take some of my vitamins."

"Okay, okay. And Maria, thanks." Michael leaned through the window, grabbed her by the waist, and pulled her a few steps closer. Then he kissed her.

Before she could even think about kissing back, he was gone. She stared after him as he trotted across her back lawn and climbed over the gate leading to the street.

Maria ran her fingers over her lips. That wasn't exactly the first kiss from Michael she'd been dreaming about. But it was a start. A grin broke across her face. It was a definite start.

Maria sat back down at her desk. She wanted to use the pen to see Valenti again right away. Maybe he had finished with Kyle and left the house. She needed to track every move he made.

Do some homework first, she told herself. Checking on Valenti every few minutes was insane. She needed to give him a little time to do something between tries.

Maria forced herself to get through her geometry problems and half the reading for social studies. Then she couldn't wait any longer. She wanted to have something to report to Michael.

Maybe he'd kiss her again if she got him some good info. A real kiss this time. One that lasted for more than half a second.

She picked up Valenti's pen. "Where is he?" she said aloud. The dots swirled, then clumped, and Maria found herself sitting in the back of the sheriff's cruiser. He was speeding down the highway, the desert stretching out on either side of him. Maria glanced around, searching for a road sign. She didn't see one.

The partition between her and Valenti dissolved into dots.

That rock, Maria thought. Remember that weird rock. A moment later she was back in her room. When the paralysis passed, she tore a clean piece of paper out of her notebook and jotted down a description of the rock she'd seen from Valenti's car. It looked sort of like a chicken. It wasn't much to go on, but it was something.

Of course, she didn't know that Valenti was even going anywhere important. He could just be joyriding through the desert, for all she knew. She decided she would wait awhile and check on him again.

Maria finished the social studies reading. She knew she should start on her *Julius Caesar* paper. It was due in a week. But she couldn't sit still any longer. She was way too hyped.

She put her favorite CD in the player and cranked it. She bopped around the room, having her own private dance party. "I'm going to find Michael's ship," she cried.

For once her mom was home. So was Kevin. But Maria knew they couldn't hear her over the blaring music. She jumped on her bed and bounced. "He's going to kiss me again. He's going to fall so in love with me."

Maria giggled. She knew she was being a total dork, but she didn't care. She kept dancing and shouting until the first song on the CD started up again. She clicked it off. She'd waited long enough. It was time to check on Valenti again.

She grabbed the pen from her desk. "Where's Sheriff Valenti?" she said. The floor under her feet dissolved and the colored dots raced around her, blowing her hair in her face. Then they clumped, and she found herself in a cement tunnel. Valenti was striding down it, his boot heels echoing in the narrow space.

The dots started to swirl again. "No!" Maria exclaimed.

She didn't want to leave yet. This was important. She could feel it. "Where's Valenti?" she cried.

The dots continued to swirl, but when they clumped, she wasn't back in her room. She was in a brightly lit corridor with the sheriff. As she watched, Valenti pulled out his wallet and showed his ID to the guard posted at the far end. The guard was dressed all in gray—just like the guard near the ship. She was so close.

Valenti, and the guard, and the corridor began to dissolve into dots. Maria let the dots re-form into her room. When the paralysis passed, she decided to take a break. She needed to rest for a minute, just for a minute. She could feel pressure building behind her eyes. She was about to get a monster headache.

But it didn't matter. Not when she was about to get some great info for Michael. Maria pulled the sheet of paper with the description of the strange rock toward her. She'd make a couple of quick notes on the tunnel and the corridor, then she'd go back.

A bright red dot fell onto the page. Then another. Am I going back to Valenti without even trying? Maria thought. But if I am, then why are the dots appearing so slowly?

Because those red dots on the page are blood, she realized suddenly. Her nose was bleeding.

Maria tilted back her head to stop the flow. This was so weird. She hadn't had a nosebleed since she was about three years old. She'd walked behind someone on the swings at the playground and gotten whacked.

She didn't have time for this right now. She had to get back to Valenti. Maria reached over to her dresser and grabbed a couple of tissues out of the box. She stuffed little pieces into her nostrils. That should stop the bleeding. If it didn't, she'd deal with it later.

She wrapped her fingers around the pen again. She pressed her free hand against her chest. She could feel the ring under her fingers. "Where is Valenti?" she asked.

Alex grabbed another dusty cardboard box and slammed it down on the top of the stack. He figured he'd sweep one half of the attic, then shove all the boxes over to the clean side and sweep the rest.

Are you ready to break down and get the ROTC thing rolling, bonehead? he asked himself. Because that's what it would take for his dad to stop coming up with work orders like this.

Alex grabbed the broom and started to sweep. He wondered what tomorrow's little job would be. He'd already cleaned the garage, the basement, and the attic. He'd done a ton of yard work, too. Maybe the Major would have him clean all the bathroom floors with a toothbrush. Alex knew there was no way he'd run out of ideas.

Being the last kid left at home sucks, Alex thought. Before his brothers had joined the military— making old dad very proud—they'd managed to do enough stupid stuff to get assigned their fair share of the grunt work.

Maybe I'll take a break and call Isabel, he thought. I should make sure she's okay. He yanked open the window and took a deep breath of the fresh air.

Oh, you're such a good friend, a little voice in his head mocked him. You want to talk to Isabel because you're so, so concerned about her. It has nothing to do with the fact that you start getting the shakes if you go too long without seeing her, just go into Isabel withdrawal.

There were footsteps on the stairs. Alex picked up the dustpan. It was probably his dad, coming to make sure he wasn't slacking off. He bent down and started to sweep his dust pile in the pan.

"Hi," a soft voice said behind him.

He glanced over his shoulder—and saw Isabel climbing into the attic with a bouquet of flowers in one hand. His heart gave its usual slam against his ribs.

"Keep doing what you were doing," Isabel said. "I'll just stand here and enjoy the view until you're done."

The view? Alex dropped the dustpan and straightened up fast. He was basically an equal opportunity kind of guy. But that didn't mean he was cool with Isabel giving him compliments on his butt.

"I can finish later," he mumbled. His face felt hot, and he prayed he wasn't blushing.

"The flowers are an apology present," Isabel explained. She thrust them into his hands. "I figured since it was my second apology in about a week, you deserved the deluxe version."

"Uh, thanks. If it's about calling me a charity case, don't worry about it. I know you were kidding." He set the flowers on the floor next to him.

"Actually, that's not what I'm apologizing for.

Although I should apologize for that, too," Isabel said.

Oh no, Alex thought. She's going to say she's sorry about crying when I kissed her! This was awful. Couldn't they both just pretend that it never happened? Why did girls have to talk about stuff so much?

"What I wanted to say is that I've been totally using you to help me get through . . . what happened," Isabel told him. "I've taken up every second of your time just because I was afraid to be alone."

"That's not using me," Alex said. "We're friends."

"But the other thing . . . you know, me thinking about Nikolas when I was kissing you and crying and everything. I do owe you an apology for that," Isabel insisted.

It was bad enough that it happened. He really, really didn't want to do some postgame analysis of it all. "Forget about it," he muttered.

"I can't forget about it," she said. "I went to the mall after school. I wanted to look at the spot where Nikolas died, to prove to myself that I could take it." Isabel pulled in a long, shuddering breath. "It was horrible, but I did it."

"That took guts," Alex told her.

She shrugged. "Anyway, after that I went around to some of the other stores, places Nikolas and I had gone right before . . ."

Alex nodded. This had to be what hell was like. Listening to Isabel tell him all her special memories about Nikolas. He knew he told her he'd be there for her. And he wanted to be. But couldn't she do this part with Liz or Maria?

"I started thinking about him. And you. And I realized if Nikolas was still alive, and you were both standing right in front of me, I'd choose you," she said in a rush.

Yeah, she thought that now that Nikolas was dead. When they had really been standing right in front of her, she'd walked away from Alex and never looked back.

"Isabel, I . . . thanks for telling me that," Alex said. "But I don't think . . . I think . . ." Can you say babbling? he asked himself. "I don't think it's a good idea for us to try to be more than friends."

"Okay. I definitely understand," Isabel answered. "I just want to give you one more thing, then I'll take off." She pulled a little strip of photos out of her purse and handed it to him.

The photos were obviously taken in the same booth as the last set. Alex recognized the faded blue background. At least Nikolas won't be in these, he thought.

Isabel leaned forward and touched the top photo. "In this one I was thinking about how you helped get Valenti away from Max—right after you found out the truth about us," she said.

She pointed to the next photo. "And in this one I was thinking about the sound of your voice when you told me all those stories. I was sitting right on the other side of the door, listening to every word."

She slid her finger down to the next picture. "This is the one where I was thinking about the way you touched me at the homecoming dance. Remember?"

Alex suddenly found it hard to breathe. Yeah, he remembered. He definitely remembered.

"And the last one, in that one I was thinking about how much I want you to kiss me again," she said.

Maybe she really meant it, he thought. Maybe she really would choose me over Nikolas.

He leaned forward slowly, then he kissed her, his lips barely brushing hers.

Isabel kept her eyes open, looking at him the whole time. At *him*.

Maria felt like someone was stabbing an ice pick into the back of her eyeballs. She couldn't get her nose to stop bleeding. But she had to hold out a little longer. Valenti was in the warehouse with the ship. She had to *see* him when he left. If she did, she might be able to give Michael the exact location of the ship, the thing he wanted most.

"Where's Valenti?" she asked, gripping the pen in both hands. The dots spun around her, making her head feel like it was about to explode. When they clumped, she was back in the warehouse. Valenti hadn't moved since last time. A few seconds later the warehouse began to dissolve into the dots, and she didn't try to stop it from happening. She would check back in a few minutes. She needed to rest.

The dots clumped, forming her room. Maria took a deep breath and realized the blood had completely soaked the tissues in her nostrils. She reached for the box of tissues on her dresser—and the paralysis hit. She couldn't stop herself from tumbling onto the floor.

Don't panic. All you have to do is wait it out, she told herself, fighting to stay calm. You're not going to get hurt lying on the floor of your own room, okay?

Maria could feel the blood dripping out of her nose and sliding down the side of her face. The sensation was driving her nuts. She wanted to reach up and wipe the blood away. But she couldn't even move her little finger.

It won't be much longer, she thought. Her eyes started to feel dry and itchy because she couldn't blink them.

Not much longer, she repeated. Her skin felt itchy, too, itchy and hot. She must have given herself a carpet burn when she fell. Except . . . except *all* of her skin felt hot. Not just the part touching the carpet.

The heat covered her body, sending pinpricks of heat into every pore.

And it was getting hotter.

Michael didn't know how he was even going to get his two hours of sleep tonight. He had to be living in the noisiest house in America. Dylan was doing his snoring thing in the other bed, and Amanda had the flu. Mr. Pascal kept bringing her into the bathroom across the hall, so Michael got to hear every moment of her puking. He felt bad for her, but still . . .

He rolled over on his side. He was going nuts. At least Sarah hadn't started her nightly scream fest. He had to be thankful for that.

Sarah must have been a mind reader because right then she started to wail. Michael heard Mrs. Pascal rushing into her room. Which meant the singing would start any second.

I'm out of here, Michael thought. With all this

going on, the Pascals probably won't even notice. And if they do, I'll deal with them—and Cuddihy—tomorrow. He crept over to the window, opened it, and crawled out.

He didn't even have to think about where to go. He headed straight for Maria's. He wanted to find out if she'd had any luck with the pen. And maybe he'd try kissing her again. That quick one hadn't brought up any little-sister feelings. Maybe he was ready to move on to the real thing and really let himself taste Maria's raspberry lips.

Michael started to jog. He loved being out at this time of night. He felt like he owned the whole town. He picked up speed, running full out, flying. He turned onto Maria's street. It was after midnight, but he knew she wouldn't mind a late visit. She never did.

Her mom's car was parked in the driveway, so he tried to be extra quiet as he climbed over the fence. He crept around to Maria's window. It was still open, so he climbed on in.

And saw her lying on the floor. A sharp acid taste flooded his mouth as he rushed over to her. Maria's blue eyes stared up at him, blank and empty. Blood was smeared under her nose and down one cheek. And tiny red dots covered her skin—her face, her neck, her arms, her hands, everywhere that he could see.

"Maria!" He took her by the shoulders and gave her a gentle shake. Her body was stiff and still under his hands. "Maria, come on! Say something." She didn't utter a sound.

He grabbed the sports bottle off her dresser and

squirted some water on her face. He stared at her intently. Move, please, you've got to, he thought. But he didn't see even the tiniest response.

He didn't think this was another spell of paralysis. There'd never been any blood before. And those red dots—what were they? What had happened to Maria?

Michael pressed his head against her chest. Relief surged through him when he heard her heart beating, fast and sort of jumpy, but definitely beating. Okay, I can deal with this, he thought, fighting to stay calm. I can heal her. I just have to make a connection. Then I'll be able to figure out what's wrong.

He took a deep breath and studied Maria's still form. He wasn't as good at healing as Max was, but he knew he could do this. He had to. There wasn't any wound that he could see, so Michael rested his hands on Maria's forehead. He focused all his attention on her. He was expecting to get a rush of images from her mind.

Instead he saw two *creatures*. Their—*faces* didn't even seem like the right word—were wide at the forehead and narrowed down to pointed chins. Their mouths were gaping circles lined with thin earthworm-length tentacles. The tentacles waved in the air, searching, searching. They had no noses and shallow, bumpy depressions where their eyes should be.

No, Michael realized. Those bumps *were* their eyes. They had dozens of eyes.

In unison the creatures swung their heads toward Michael. The tentacles of their mouths stretched toward him, straining to reach him.

They see me, Michael realized. He jerked his hands away from Maria. He felt like his whole body was vibrating. His teeth kept knocking together.

What was that? What the hell was going on? Those . . . *things* weren't any memory of Maria's. And they saw him. It was impossible, but it happened.

Max. He had to call Max. Michael leaped to his feet and snatched Maria's phone off her dresser. He punched in the Evanses' number. Isabel answered on the second ring. "I need you and Max to get over to Maria's right away," Michael said. "And be quiet. I don't want her mom or her little brother waking up."

If Mrs. DeLuca saw Maria right now, she'd call an ambulance. And that would be a big mistake. Michael didn't know what was happening to Maria, but there was no way any hospital or doctor could deal with it. And while they were trying to figure out what to do, Maria could die.

Michael suddenly felt like he'd chugged a gallon of ice water. Coldness rushed through his body, cramping his stomach, making him ache.

That's not going to happen. Don't even think that, he ordered himself. Maria is not going to die. I won't let her.

"What happened?" Isabel exclaimed.

"Just get here," Michael ordered, keeping his voice low. He hung up the phone and returned to Maria. He sat down next to her. "You're going to be all right," he said softly. "I'm going to take care of you. I'm going to figure out a way to heal you."

He reached out and slid his palm down over her

eyes, forcing the lids to close. He hated seeing her eyes all blank like that.

Michael decided he should go wait by the front door for Max and Isabel. It's not like they could ring the doorbell or anything. That would definitely wake up Maria's mom and brother.

He leaned close to Maria, her soft hair brushing against his face. Her skin felt hot under his fingers, way too hot. "I have to go away for a minute," he whispered. "But I'll be right back." Then he kissed her. Her lips were soft and sweet, just like he'd thought they'd be.

"I should have done that before," he told her. Then Michael pushed himself to his feet and crept through the dark house to the front door. He unlocked it and stepped out onto the front porch. He'd wait for Max and Isabel out there.

But he couldn't stand still. He hurried out into the middle of the street and looked for Max's Jeep. Where was he? Didn't he know this was an emergency?

You talked to Isabel about two seconds ago, Michael reminded himself. They'll be here as fast as they can.

Michael wondered if he had time to check on Maria and get back out here before they showed up. He turned back toward the house and caught sight of a pair of headlights out of the corner of his eye. He stared down the street. Yeah, it was the Jeep. Max had obviously broken a few speed limits to get here.

Max pulled up alongside him. "What's going on?" he demanded.

148

"It's Maria. She's in a coma or something. When I made the connection to heal her, I saw two creatures, I don't even know what to call them, staring at me. They saw me. I know it," Michael explained, his words tumbling on top of each other.

"Okay, we need a plan," Isabel said, her voice calm and steady. "We are going to come up with a way to save her—now."

"Let's take her to Ray's," Max said. "His powers of healing might be stronger than ours."

Ray wasn't exactly Michael's favorite person. But if he could help Maria, Michael would get down on his knees and kiss the guy's feet.

"I'll go get her," Michael said. "You two wait here. There's more chance we'll get caught if we all go." He ran back to the front door and slipped inside. He made his way back to Maria's room and scooped her up in his arms. He cradled her tight against his chest. She still felt so hot. He didn't know if that was good or bad. At least it meant she was still alive.

He carried her out of the house and over to the Jeep. He climbed into the backseat, still holding her. "We're going to take care of you," he said. He hoped somehow she could hear him.

Max pulled the Jeep out of the driveway and peeled out down the street. Isabel twisted around and ran her fingers down Maria's cheek. "Something weird happened with Maria a couple of days ago," she told Michael. "We were in English, and she had a little spell or something. Like a blackout. When I asked her what happened, she wouldn't tell me."

Michael gave a growl of frustration. "That happened when she was with me, too. I should have known she was hurting herself. She looked like she was half dead when she was paralyzed."

"What are you talking about?" Max demanded.

"Maria's psychic. Every time she uses her power, she gets paralyzed. Can't move, can't talk, nothing. She made it sound like it was no big deal. But she couldn't see herself when it was happening. If she could—" Michael broke off and shoved his fingers through his hair.

"Psychic? Are you sure?" Isabel exclaimed.

Max pulled into the UFO museum parking lot and parked the Jeep at the foot of the stairs leading to Ray's apartment. "Do you want help with her?" he asked Michael.

"No. No, you go ahead. Tell Ray what happened. I'll be right behind you." Max and Isabel jumped out of the Jeep and took off up the stairs.

Michael climbed out of the Jeep and took the stairs more slowly, trying to jar Maria as little as possible. "Ray's going to know how to help you," he told her. He wanted her to know what was happening.

Ray met him at the front door. "Put her down in the living room and let me look at her," he said.

Max shoved a couple of the beanbags together, and Michael carefully laid Maria on top of them. He sat on the floor nearby, keeping her hand locked in his.

Ray knelt down next to them. His eyes were wide as he stared at her. With a shaking hand he lightly touched one of the red spots on Maria's face.

"Bounty hunters," he whispered.

"What?" Michael demanded.

Isabel joined them in the living room. "I called Alex. He's going to get Liz and come over."

Ray grabbed Michael by the arm, his fingers squeezing hard. "Max said you saw some kind of creatures when you connected with Maria. Did they have multiple eyes and tentacle mouths?"

"Yeah. Why? What's going on? Can you help her?" Michael asked.

"The things you saw . . . they're bounty hunters. A race of creatures from our planet," Ray explained. "Their bodies are designed for hunting, and our people used them to track down criminals. They use a kind of . . . mental warfare. It leaves spots like the ones on Maria."

"Mental warfare? What's that?" Isabel demanded.

"It's something the hunters use to kill from a great distance," Ray answered. "They use their minds as weapons. Their power is staggering."

"*Kill?*" Michael exploded. "Someone's trying to kill Maria?"

"It looks that way," Ray said.

"But you're saying an alien did this," Max jumped in. "Why would an alien target Maria?"

"Good question," Ray said. "I don't—"

"I have a better question," Michael interrupted. "How do we stop them? What do we have to do to save Maria?" He stared down at her face—and saw her eyelids flutter. "She moved!" he cried.

He rubbed her hand between his. "Maria, can

you hear me?" Michael demanded. "Are you okay?"

Her eyes slowly opened. They had lost their horrible blank expression. "Thirsty," she mumbled.

"I'll get water," Isabel said.

Michael brushed Maria's hair away from her face. He smoothed her shirt down over her stomach. He couldn't seem to stop touching her. "You scared me," he said.

"Sorry." Maria's voice was thick and scratchy. Isabel rushed back in and handed Michael a glass of water. He wrapped one arm around Maria's shoulders and helped her sit up enough to drink.

"Do you feel well enough to tell us what happened?" Ray asked.

"I don't know what happened. How did I get here? What—" She was interrupted by a frantic pounding on the front door.

"I got it," Max said. He hurried out of the room and returned a moment later followed by Alex and Liz.

"Are you okay, Maria?" Liz cried.

"What happened?" Alex half yelled.

"I stopped by Maria's and found her passed out on the floor," Michael explained. "She had these red spots all over her."

Maria raised her hand in front of her face. She gave a soft whimper when she saw the spots.

Michael tightened his arm around her. He knew it was going to be really hard for her to hear the rest. "Ray says alien bounty hunters were after her." He locked eyes with Maria. "They're using some kind of

152

mental weapon on you, but we're going to figure out a way to stop them. Right?" he asked Ray.

Ray didn't give Michael the answer he wanted. He didn't say he knew exactly how to stop the bounty hunters. He just smiled at Maria. "First I think we need more information," he said. "Tell me about your psychic powers—and the spells you get."

"She doesn't have any psychic powers," Liz burst out.

Maria looked up at Liz. "Actually, I do. I was going to tell you. I just—"

"Maria," Alex said gently, "just tell us the facts."

"I . . . I found a ring in the mall, a ring with a strange stone," she said slowly.

A ring? Michael thought. Maria hadn't told him about that.

She cleared her throat, and Michael gave her another sip of water. "The stone helped me tap into psychic powers I didn't even know I had. Healing. And I could touch any object and then *see* the person it belonged to—know exactly what they were doing right at that second."

Michael could feel Maria trembling. But she was holding it together, telling them what they needed to know.

"Can I see the ring?" Ray asked.

Maria pulled the gold chain off her neck and handed it to Ray. A ring set with a green-purple stone hung on the end.

Ray ran one finger over the stone. "It's one of the Stones of Midnight," he said, his voice hushed and solemn. "I never thought I would hold one in my hand."

Isabel leaned over for a look. "That's Nikolas's ring!" she cried.

"I found it the night . . . the night he, you know," Maria said. "I didn't know it was his."

It was good to hear her talking. Plus her skin was cooler and those little red dots were gone. He'd been so afraid . . . Michael didn't even want to complete the thought.

"How could Nikolas have gotten the Stone?" Max asked.

"The Stone was stolen by the stowaway on our ship," Ray reminded them. "Maybe someone found it at the crash site. Or somehow it was attached to Nikolas's pod—"

"Who cares about that right now," Michael snapped. "We have to stay focused on Maria."

"Well, now I know why the bounty hunters have targeted Maria," Ray said. "They're after the Stone. The consortium must have hired them to track down the fugitive and retrieve it."

Ray ran his fingers through his thinning gray-brown hair. "Every time Maria used the power of the Stone—what she thought was her psychic power—she was sending a signal to the bounty hunters, helping them track her down. They've obviously gotten close enough to begin using mental warfare against her."

Maria cleared her throat again. "Wouldn't they be able to tell I wasn't an alien?" she asked.

"Not necessarily," Ray answered. "The hunters are

probably still too far away to tell anything except that the Stone is being used."

"So if Maria stops using the Stone, it's over, right?" Michael asked. "If she doesn't use it, she doesn't send out a signal, and the bounty hunters can't find her, right?"

"I don't think they'll be able to find Maria if she doesn't use the Stone again," Ray agreed.

"Good. Problem solved. I'm taking her home," Michael said.

He decided he would sleep on her floor. No, not sleep. Lie on her floor and watch her, make sure she was okay.

"I'm fine," Maria protested. But she sounded awful. And Michael was pretty sure if he moved his arm, she wouldn't be able to hold herself upright.

"What I'm afraid of is that the bounty hunters may have been able to target Maria's general location," Ray added. "If they can't find her, they may decide to do something drastic—like destroy the whole town. That way they'd be sure of killing her. And the Stone would still be safe. There isn't a weapon that can destroy it."

"So we get in the Jeep right now and get as far away as possible," Michael said.

"And leave everyone else to die?" Liz exclaimed. "I don't think so."

"I was so stupid. I actually thought I had some kind of special power. I thought the Stone was just helping me use it," Maria cried.

"It wasn't stupid. Were you supposed to think you'd found an alien power stone in the *mall?*" Liz asked.

"So we need a plan," Alex said. "Anyone have any ideas?"

"Remember how we got our friend the sheriff off Max's trail right after he healed me?" Liz asked. "We convinced Valenti the alien he was looking for was dead. Could we pull the same kind of thing on the bounty hunters?"

"Yeah, if they thought I was dead, they'd stop trying to kill me—and there would be no reason for them to hurt anyone else," Maria said.

"There is a way . . . but it's dangerous," Max answered.

Dangerous. That was not a word Michael wanted to hear in connection with Maria.

"Maria could use the ring to call the bounty hunters to her," Max continued. "Then I'll use my power to stop her heart. Just for a few seconds, just long enough to convince the bounty hunters she's dead. Then I could start it again."

Fury slammed through Michael. How could Max even think about putting Maria in that kind of situation? "There is no way I'm letting you do something like that," he spat out.

Maria tightened her grip on his hand. "It's not your decision. It's mine," she said firmly. "And I'm doing it."

Maria stared down at her arm. She wished the red dots would reappear. When the dots came back, that would mean the bounty hunters had targeted her again—and that she could get this over with. She hated the waiting, knowing that soon she was going to die.

"Are you okay?" Liz asked. "We should have let you rest more first."

"This way it will make it easier for Max to kill me," she said. She meant it to come out light and teasing. But Max stiffened, Liz turned pale, and a shiver ran through Maria's body.

"If Max and Michael and Ray screw up, don't worry," Isabel jumped in. "You've still got me. I'll bring you back."

"I don't think talking about screwing up is *helpful* right now," Alex said.

"No, it's . . . I appreciate it," Maria answered. She did, too. It meant a lot that Isabel was willing to heal her even though she'd sworn never to use her powers again. "Thanks. Thanks, Izzy."

"I still don't think—," Michael began.

"I'm going to use the Stone again," Maria announced.

She couldn't stand waiting. "I used it a bunch of times in a row the last time."

Maria wrapped her fingers around the bracelet she'd borrowed from her mother. "What's Mom doing?" she whispered.

The dots swirled, then clumped. And Maria found herself standing in her mother's bedroom. Her mom was asleep, a small smile on her lips. What if I never see her again? Maria thought.

The dots started to swirl. "I love you, Mom," Maria called. Then the dots clumped and she was back in Ray's living room. The paralysis struck immediately this time. Maria could see and hear everything, just like she had when Michael held her in his arms and told her everything was all right, when he kissed her.

"It's time," she heard Alex say. "There are dots on her arms."

Think of Michael. Keep thinking of Michael, she told herself. That would help get her through the next few minutes.

Max stood up and crossed the room to her. Maria felt her heart flutter in her chest—like it knew what was about to happen. Like it knew it was going to be forced to stop beating. He knelt down next to her.

"Don't touch her," Michael ordered.

"Michael, there's no other—," Liz began to protest.

"I'll do it," Michael said. He took a deep breath and pressed his hands against her chest. She knew he was getting ready to make the connection. In a few seconds she'd be dead.

Michael lowered his head so his eyes were only inches from her own. "Don't think about anything but me," he told her.

She wished she could tell him that's what she'd *been* doing.

Michael's eyes never left hers as he slid his hands up from her chest to her throat. Was he having trouble making the connection? "Just think of me," he murmured.

Maria felt his hand slide through her hair and then—Michael tore the gold chain from around her neck.

"What are you doing?" Alex cried.

Michael shoved the ring onto his finger and sprang to his feet. "I want to be the one to die," he announced.

"We have to stick to the plan," Max said urgently.

"No," Michael answered. "End of discussion." He curled his hand into a fist. "No one is taking this ring off me. So either you use me instead of Maria or the plan fails."

No! Maria wanted to scream at them to stop. But she couldn't get out even a word.

"They're connecting with me now," Michael announced. He held out his arm, showing everyone the red dots. Max rushed over to Michael. He shoved his hands down on Michael's chest.

A shudder ripped through Maria's body as the paralysis broke. She sat up fast. "Don't do it!" Maria wailed. This wasn't right. She should be the one to die.

But it was too late. Michael crumpled to the floor.

His body gave two jerks and then lay still. Maria could see little bubbles of foam on his lips.

"Max, what did you do?" Isabel yelled.

Max stumbled away from Michael's body. "I didn't do anything. I didn't even get a chance to make the connection."

"Is he dead?" Maria cried. "Is Michael dead?"

15

"I don't know what happened. I didn't even make it *in*," Max cried.

Isabel pushed her way past him and dropped down next to Michael's body. She placed her hands on his chest.

You can do this, she told herself. You have the power. Just relax and focus on Michael. Only on Michael. She took a few deep breaths and waited for the flood of images from Michael's brain. They didn't come.

She wasn't going to let him die. She couldn't save Nikolas. She'd been too terrified to even try. She'd just stood there and watched Valenti shoot him. But she wasn't going to stand around and let Michael die. She was going to save him.

Isabel pulled up his T-shirt and repositioned her hands on his bare skin. Skin-to-skin contact always helped her make the connection. She closed her eyes, willing herself to keep her breathing slow and steady. She knew if she got tense and tried to force things, it would only make the connection harder to achieve.

The images still didn't come. Maybe her power had gotten dulled because she hadn't been using it.

161

She opened her eyes. "Max, you've got to help me. I can't make the connection," Isabel told him.

Max crouched down next to Michael and positioned his hands on either side of Isabel's. "Let's try together," he said.

They had known Michael their whole lives. They loved him. If anyone could connect with him, they could. So this had to work. It had to.

Isabel listened to Max's deep breathing and matched her breaths to his. She starting running through all the moments with Michael she had stored in her brain.

"Something's happening," Alex said softly. "Look at Michael."

Isabel stared down at him and saw a sickly gray glow forming around his body. That had never happened during a healing before. Was it a good sign or a bad one?

"Let's see what a little more juice can do," Ray said. He knelt next to Max and put his hands on Michael's forehead. The light around Michael grew a little brighter.

Then it flickered and went out.

"Come on, Max. What are you waiting for?" Michael demanded. "You've got to do this now. Before it's too late."

Max didn't answer. No one answered. The room was completely still and silent. Even the clock had stopped ticking.

Michael opened his eyes and sat up. Max, Maria, Isabel, Alex, Liz, and Ray—they had all disappeared.

What was going on? He stumbled to his feet, fighting against a wave of dizziness. "Where are you guys?" Michael shouted.

He rushed to the front door and threw it open. He took the stairs two at a time. Max's Jeep was still parked in the UFO museum lot. He could see it clearly. But . . . but everything outside the lot was covered in a thick mist.

"Max! Maria! Anyone! Are you out there? Can you hear me?" Michael yelled.

Again he got no answer. But something was moving deep in the mist. Something was coming toward him.

Michael squinted into the mist. Two figures began to form—tall and thin, with incredibly long arms and legs. They moved closer and he got a glimpse of their faces. It was them. The bounty hunters.

"You're just the guys I've been hoping to run into," Michael yelled. He was going to show them exactly why they shouldn't have messed with someone he cared about.

He locked his eyes on one of the bounty hunters and ran straight at him. He tackled the hunter and knocked him to the ground. He grabbed the hunter's head and smashed it against the asphalt. He lifted it up and smashed it again. He did not want the guy getting back up—ever.

The second bounty hunter yanked Michael away. Michael landed hard on his back, the breath rushing out of his lungs with a *whoosh*. The hunter pressed his fingers against Michael's stomach. Instantly a connection between them formed. Michael felt the hunter's mind probe his internal organs—and begin ripping a hole in Michael's stomach. He could feel the hot gastric enzymes spilling into his body cavity.

"You want to play, let's play," Michael muttered. He did a quick check of the hunter's body. He could see the organs and muscles and tissue. He spotted an unfamiliar gland at the base of the throat. Let's see what this little baby does, Michael thought. He focused his attention on it and *squeezed* with his mind.

He felt the hunter rip another hole in his stomach. Michael squeezed his eyes shut as more acid flooded his body. Enough fooling around, he thought. He didn't see anything in the hunter's body that looked exactly like a heart. But he figured that pulsing thing where his liver should be must do something important.

He focused on it and crushed the cells together. He tried to imagine that he was a trash compactor and the heart thing was an aluminum can. He gave it another good squeeze. And it stopped beating.

Michael pushed the hunter off him and pressed his hands against his stomach. He nudged the molecules of the gastric acid, urging them farther and farther apart. The burning in his stomach lessened until it felt like he'd just eaten too many chili dogs with lemon.

Michael caught a twitch of movement out of the corner of his eye. It was the first bounty hunter. *He lived?*

Time for round two. Michael shoved himself to his feet and took a step toward the first hunter. He heard a wet, squishing sound, and the hunter's body split in two.

Both halves stood up and turned toward Michael, their dozens and dozens of eyes locked on him.

Michael backed away and stumbled over the hunter still on the ground. Before he could move, they were on him. One latched onto the biggest artery in Michael's brain. The other went for his heart.

Red dots exploded in front of Michael's eyes. Then everything went black.

Maria moaned as the light around Michael went dark. This couldn't be happening. She wasn't going to *let* this happen.

But what could she do? She was back to being an ordinary girl. She didn't have any power.

"Michael, don't give up!" Maria cried. At least she could let him know she was there. Let him know she cared about him. Maybe somehow he'd be able to hear her, the way she'd heard him.

Liz slipped her arm around Maria's shoulders. "Yeah, come on, Michael. You've got to fight. I know you're a fighter."

Alex wrapped one arm around her and one around Liz. "You've got to come back, Michael. You still owe me two bucks!"

At least her friends were here with her. Maria didn't know what she'd do if she had to go through this alone.

That's it! she thought. I couldn't do it alone. None of us can do it *alone*.

She rushed over and squeezed between Max and Isabel. She grabbed each of their hands in hers. "Alex, Liz, come on. Form a circle—like we did that night in the cave."

Liz and Alex didn't ask questions. They quickly joined the group around Michael. Liz took Ray's hand and then linked hands with Alex. Alex locked fingers with Max. Ray reached out and took Isabel's hand.

The moment the circle of hands was complete, bands of color wrapped themselves around Michael. The sparkling blue emanating from Maria, the emerald green from Max, the bright orange from Alex, the rich amber from Liz, the deep purple from Isabel, and the creamy, almost colorless light from Ray.

Tears streamed down Maria's face. This had to work. What she had felt that night in the cave, the night Max had formed a connection between them, was the most powerful experience of her life. Stronger and deeper than anything she'd felt using the Stone. If the force of the group connection wasn't enough to save Michael, then it was over. He was dead.

"Come on, Michael. Come back to us," Max cried.

"Don't you dare walk away from me," Isabel added.

"I love you, Michael," Maria whispered.

They waited.

"Concentrate, everyone," Maria begged her friends.

She could feel Max's death grip on her left hand, and Isabel's nails digging into her right hand.

Slowly, slowly, a new color appeared, mixed with the bands of blue, green, orange, purple, amber, and white. The brick red of Michael's aura. It grew brighter and brighter until it soaked the room, throwing red light on everything.

Michael opened his eyes. "Can't you get along for one second without me?" he mumbled.

"Are you sure this is safe?" Maria asked. She kept a tight grip on Michael's hand. She didn't think she'd ever let go.

"It's the only way," Ray replied. "I don't want to put it back out in the world where some other innocent human might find it. And nothing on this planet could destroy it. If I keep the Stone here, it will be safe."

"You won't use it?" Michael pressed. "I don't want my 'death' to go to waste. Those bounty hunters were nasty."

"I'll never use it," Ray promised. "How about another Lime Warp?"

"I'd love one," Michael said.

When Ray headed into the kitchen, Maria turned to Michael. "Are you sure you're okay? You didn't really tell us what happened."

Michael's beautiful eyes took on a pained expression. "I don't want to talk about it," he murmured. "They killed me, I know it. I was dead. I don't know how you saved me."

Isabel took Michael's other hand and smiled at Maria. "Teamwork," she said gently. "Turns out we *all* need powers."

"No," Maria corrected her. "We all need each other."

"That was pretty intense," Liz commented to Max as they started down the stairs to the parking lot. "I have to say, my life's gotten a lot more exciting since we became . . . friends."

Max winced. "Maybe we should stay away from each other completely," he said. "Even being friends might be too—"

"Stop." Liz grabbed him by the arm and pulled him around to face her. "Don't even say that. Didn't you feel what happened in there? Do you think that would have happened with just any group of people? There's something special between us . . . between all of us. You can't throw it away."

Max stared down into her eyes for a long moment. "You're right." He slipped his arms around her, pulling her against him.

Liz leaned into the embrace, resting her cheek on his chest. Even if they were just friends, she could stay like this forever. Just holding Max, feeling his heart beat.

His heart . . . it didn't sound right. Didn't sound strong.

Max's arms dropped away from her. Liz watched, terrified, as his eyes rolled up into his head. He slumped to the ground.

"Max?" she cried. *"Max!"*

ROSWELL
HIGH

SOME SECRETS ARE TOO DANGEROUS TO KNOW...

Don't miss Roswell High #4
The Watcher

Max is dying. No one wants to believe it, but he knows it's true. And as the end grows closer, he can only think of one thing: Who will protect Liz if he's not there?

Liz can't stand watching Max suffer. She's determined to find some way – any way – to save him. But the only way to help Max is to risk her own life. Is she willing to die for the one she loves?

Look out for Roswell High #5
The Intruder
Coming soon from Pocket Books!

F E A R L E S S™

. . . a girl born without the fear gene

Seventeen-year-old Gaia Moore is not your typical high school senior. She is a black belt in karate, was doing advanced maths in junior school and, oh yes, she absolutely Does Not Care. About anything. Her mother is dead and her father, a covert anti-terrorist agent, abandoned her years ago. But before he did, he taught her self-preservation. Tom Moore knew there would be a lot of people after Gaia because of who, and what, she is. Gaia is genetically enhanced not to feel fear and her life has suddenly become dangerous. Her world is about to explode with terrorists, government spies and psychos bent on taking her apart. But Gaia does not care. She is Fearless.